HOPE

Project Middle School

HOPE

Project Middle School

By Alyssa Milano
with Debbie Rigaud
ILLUSTRATED BY ERIC S. KEYES

Scholastic Inc.

Library of Congress Cataloging-in-Publication Data Available

ISBN 978-1-338-32940-7

10 9 8 7 6 5 4 3 2 1   19 20 21 22 23

Printed in the U.S.A.   23

First printing 2019
Book design by Katie Fitch

This book is dedicated to Milo and Bella.
You give me hope. I'm so proud to be your mom.
—A.M.

For Olivia and Lincoln.
—D.R.

To my son, Ollie.
—E.K.

Chapter 1

"**H**i, I'm—*Whoa!*"

Cosmo leaps into my lap and props his tiny paws on my shoulders. I crack up, sinking deeper into the couch cushions.

"Okay, buddy. You can be in the video, too. Say hi, Cosmo!" I wave to the camera recording us from the coffee table. We look cute together—my big hair, his shaggy fur. And who can resist those pleading puppy dog eyes?

"Hey, it's me—Hope Roberts, future scientist. Welcome to my first-ever video journal! Guess what?" I pause for effect, and Cosmo waits with bated—and dog—breath. "Tomorrow I start sixth grade! Yes, me at JFK Middle School! My hypothesis is that life as I know it will change. So, before that happens, I want to take you on a tour of my world. This is my home."

I stand up and wave my Cosmo-free arm like, *Ta-da!* Our other dog, a giant mutt named Rocket, is busy gnawing a bone and has zero desire to be on camera.

Just then, a howl comes from down the hall, setting off Cosmo, so he's howling, too. I set him down, away from my eardrum. "Cosmo . . . *ssshh!*" It's useless. The noise is bothering him just as much as it's bothering me.

"First scientific observation," I say, going down the hall, past Rocket and toward the sound. "There is a terrible whining coming from an unknown source. And no, we don't have a third dog."

The sound gets louder and more irritating as I head down the hallway. I stop at my sister's bedroom. Marie is inside—singing. (If you can call it that.)

"Aha! Sound origin found." Her door is ajar, but I nudge it open wider.

Her polka-dot headphones are on, but she tears them off and storms over when she notices me peeking in.

"What do you want? Can't you read?" Marie points to the KEEP OUT! sign on her door. She crosses her arms and stares me down, her attitude switched on.

I bravely continue documenting my observations. "Witness a teenager in her natural habitat. Imagine being buried in the trendiest clothes and painted with layers of makeup, all while swinging from one wild mood to another. Highly fascinating."

Marie scrunches up her face. "Who are you even filming that for?"

"For myself, a future Nobel Prize committee, extraterrestrials . . . There could be anyone on the other side of this camera. That's what makes this so great, don't you think?"

"You sound like Dad," Marie groans, like that's uncool.

"Excellent!" I respond. Dad can never be uncool. He's a rocket scientist who works at NASA! True story. I'm seriously not being ironic when I say that!

Our mom is pretty awesome, too. She's super smart and owns a downtown gallery full of masterpieces—some of which she buys for our walls. But she says

her favorite piece of all is our family photo. Mom's just being sweet, because clearly there's a piece of spinach stuck in Dad's teeth. (Okay, maybe occasionally he can be uncool.) Dental don'ts aside, I want to follow in his footsteps when I grow up.

"Whatever." Marie is tired of my documenting and slams the door in my face.

"Welp. I guess that counts as today's quality time together. Let's venture into friendlier territory, shall we?" I take a few steps across the hallway.

"Here we are in my room, which I use as a science lab when I need to." I pan the camera past the poufy planet pillows and pops of pink to a wooden

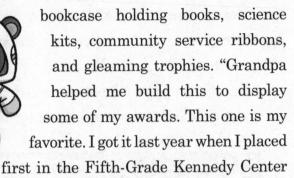

bookcase holding books, science kits, community service ribbons, and gleaming trophies. "Grandpa helped me build this to display some of my awards. This one is my favorite. I got it last year when I placed first in the Fifth-Grade Kennedy Center Robotics Fair." I zoom in on the towering winning trophy. "I built a mini-rocket prototype that launched almost five hundred feet into the air. All on my own," I say for good measure, still bothered by the kids who assumed my dad must have helped me. But they don't know Hope Roberts. Science is my superpower.

"Oh, I almost forgot! This is *so* important." I whip the camera to the shelf below, where a stack of comic books are displayed, covers facing out.

"Galaxy Girl. The *best* comic book series of all time. Galaxy Girl is like a young Wonder Woman meets Dr.

Who meets Bill Nye the Science Guy," I announce breathlessly. "She's my age and she goes on interplanetary missions! It sounds like a stretch, but believe me, she and I have so much in common.

"We both love science. And we both believe girls can do little and big things that can change the world—er, or universe. My missions have more to do with good deeds and stuff and less to do with facing off against interplanetary villains, but you get the idea. Plus, Galaxy Girl has this awesome catchphrase, which I totally live by: 'Be the brightest star.' Seriously, I can spend a whole day rereading all these comic books."

My eyes catch something over on my desk. I set

the camera down so that it's angled at the perfect shot of the space. I pick up the paper that's captured my focus. "But lately, there's only one thing I want to read over and over: this letter from JFK Middle School announcing that I've been placed in their advanced classes."

I examine it again and feel a shiver of anticipation run through me. The words "welcome" and "accelerated academic classes" stand out.

"This is, like, *huge* news. JFK Middle has the most impressive advanced program. Their science club teams run circles around everyone at the state science competitions. I've been a fan since the first grade. Since then, I've been working hard to make sure I get into their top-tier classes. And finally, now I'm in! *Squee!*" I hop up and down and squeal some more.

Cosmo and Rocket run into my room and bowl me over. I tumble to the floor laughing. It's no wonder my dad thinks they consider me their human mom. Rocket gives me a bear hug and Cosmo yaps like he's saying, *Stop staring at that letter and let's play!*

Careful not to crumble this very special document, I untangle myself from the dogs. I put the letter on

my desk but far away from Rocket. You never know when she'll be on the hunt for a papery snack. It's safe behind my framed photo of Sam. Rocket doesn't get along with her because Sam plays keep-away with her treats. Sam thinks it's the most hilarious thing.

Oh yeah—Sam! I grab Sam's picture and show it to the camera.

"This is Samantha Bowers, my best friend in the universe. She and I have been joined at the hip since pre-K! But this year, we'll be in separate classes."

Before I know it, I'm sitting on my bed, lost in thought, holding Sam's picture.

From neighboring naptime cots to joint class presentations, Sam and I have always been a team. But she wasn't selected for the accelerated classes, so we won't see much of each other at school.

We've never not been in the same class. How will this even work?

Something crinkly rings out, snapping me out of

the bummed zone. Rocket is trying to shake open one of the individually wrapped snacks I keep for her in my basket of pet toys. Taking pity on her, I unwrap it and throw the treat for her to catch. She misses. It lands closer to Cosmo, who gobbles it up right away.

"Not nice, Cosmo. You know Rocket gets *hangry* when you do that." I laugh and shake my head, already feeling better.

"One last thing! Check out the outfit I've picked for tomorrow!" I race over to my closet and lay out each item across my bed. "A denim skirt swiped from Marie's closet (*sshhh!*); a puffy pink vest, because . . . why not?; and a cosmic-cool top to rep for STEM girls everywhere. Mom's even letting me borrow her vintage backpack from when she was a teenager. How cool is that?!"

There's one more item I need from the closet—my swimsuit.

"Signing off for now. Sam is on her way over! We've planned to spend the last day of summer vacation hanging out at our pool. Until next video, feel free to form your own scientific hypothesis about me. And keep your fingers crossed for a positive and enlightening new school year!"

Ding-dong!

"Gotta run. That's Sam, right on time!"

☆

Chapter 2

"**F**irst!" Sam shouts victoriously as she slaps her hand on the pool deck.

I seriously can't hate. My best friend just may be the Florida champ of floatie racing. Or she at least has the Cape Canaveral title. She pushed the flamingo floatie to the opposite end of the pool in record time.

I come in a distant second, as usual. This, after my best efforts to use my ginormous floatie to bump her off course, splashing us both.

We're laughing and sputtering at the same time. Once we finally collapse onto our winning (or losing) floaties, we crack up a little more.

"I'll win the rematch for sure," I say while catching my breath.

"You say that every time."

I'm too comfy to be a sore loser. My float is so large and billowy, it's practically a waterproof air mattress. Marie and I always get into a tug-of-war over who gets to lie on it. But because Cosmo and Rocket like to hop on with me, I usually win.

Sam's float suits her, because she kinda reminds me of a flamingo. And not just because plastic lawn flamingos dot the front yard of her house. For one,

Sam has great balance and is super graceful, thanks to years of ballet training. But like a flamingo's bright pink feathers, Sam has a quirky side, too.

There was the time in fourth grade when she wore fairy wings to school, simply because she felt like it. Only Sam could've gotten away with that for as many classes as she did before a teacher finally asked her to take them off. I smile thinking about that day. I wonder if kids in middle school are too mature to pull silly stunts with their friends. I hope not.

The chorus of bugs chirping in surround sound makes summer feel like it's here to stay. It's past sunset, yet the air is still so hot and muggy.

"If tomorrow is going to feel this hot, I may have to change my first-day outfit," says Sam.

"But it looks so cute on you," I say, remembering the at-home fashion show we'd held at Sam's last weekend.

"Thank you." She does a happy seat-dance. "I hope Josh thinks so, too."

"Who's Josh?" I ask teasingly.

"Burger Boy," she says.

My mouth forms an O. "Burger Boy's name is Josh?" All summer, I've been hearing about this cute boy who eats neatly stacked burgers for lunch.

Sam nods and beams. "I found out on the last day of camp when he was called up onstage for an award."

The boys at my science camp were cute enough, but I didn't pay as close attention to them as Sam did to boys at her theater camp.

"Now all I need to do is find out his star sign," she says.

"What for?"

"Duh. Josh is coming to JFK Middle, too, and I'm pretty sure I'll bump into him. I'm taking inspiration from Isla, the character I played in our summer stage show. She wouldn't want any meet-cute to happen when Mercury is in retrograde. She'd do some zodiac research first."

I'm confused. And I'm rarely confused when the topic is Mercury or any other planet. "What does that even mean?"

"Only that it can ruin everything. Things went from bad to worse for Isla when Mercury was in retrograde. In this one scene, she was at home making breakfast, thinking everything is normal— and then *zap!* The power went out as she was toasting a waffle." Sam is really into the explanation. She leans in with bulging green eyes and wiggling fingers.

I'm totally sucked in. It's like watching a cool sci-fi movie.

"If it weren't for the morning sun, she would've been standing in the complete dark," she continues ominously. "But she decided to eat her waffle anyway—and then *yeouch!* The toaster was hotter than she expected and it burned her finger. She was so startled by the pain, her phone dropped out of her hand—and then *ugh*, her screen got totally shattered!"

I'm actually pretty spooked. But I still don't get her point. It makes no scientific sense. The only thing Sam's convinced me of is that she should definitely join JFK Middle's drama club. The girl is a natural.

"Instead of worrying about what Mercury is up to, why don't you run an experiment?"

"Hope, I can think of better ways to break the ice with Josh than to launch one of your homemade bottle rockets."

"I'm talking about a social experiment. Like, grab a seat next to him at lunch and see how he responds."

"Nope. My horoscope this week specifically says to avoid lunch meetings."

"Are you serious?" I giggle, thinking she's making a joke. "Or are you just being *sooo* spacey?" When she doesn't smile, I realize she's being serious. "I've never heard you talk about astrology before. Where are you getting this stuff?"

"Since the show had a lot of astrology in it, the summer camp had someone come in and read our signs," Sam says. "It really helped us find our characters. For example, I had no idea that Aquariuses were independent and social butterflies, but also wildly unpredictable. That totally describes me!"

I blink. "But you realize that could be describing anybody."

"You're not unpredictable," Sam says.

"Oh yeah?" I counter. "Guess what I had for lunch today."

"A tuna fish sandwich and apple juice," Sam says without missing a beat.

Darn. She's right. She really does know me.

"No, I drank orange juice," I fib to prove my point.

"See? Unpredictable."

Sam doesn't answer, so I lean back on my raft again to look up at the stars. But it's bothering me that we're disagreeing on something. We never disagree on anything.

"There's no scientific proof that the stars' movements have any impact on our lives, you know," I tell her.

"I think there's a lot that we don't know in the universe," Sam replies thoughtfully, pointing to the sky. "You are always saying there's more than one way to be a girl. Well, maybe there's more than one way to view the stars."

I bunch up my lips, doubtful. "I don't know."

"And you like to say we use only ten percent of our brains. What if there's ninety percent of the universe that we don't understand, too?"

"You're just throwing numbers out there like they're facts," I say. "Don't mean to get all *Myth Buster* on you, but that's made-up science. There's actually a name for it. It's called science fiction."

"Like your Galaxy Girl comics?" Sam quips.

"That's different," I say. "I don't read Galaxy Girl because it's factual. I read it because it's fun."

"Well, you'll have to check and see if the other kids in your advanced classes think I'm right," Sam finishes. She doesn't even glance my way as she speaks.

An awkward silence falls between us, just like it did when I first called her to tell her I'd gotten the letter and she said she hadn't. I feel bad. Not because I made it into the advanced classes—I'm

really proud of that. But because I wanted Sam to get the letter, too. She's a really good student when she puts her mind to it. And it's not like I got in without her on purpose. But what I am supposed to do?

"I wish we were going to be in the same classes together," I say quietly after a minute. "It's not going to be the same."

Sam takes a deep breath. "I think it will be okay. You'll be fine."

"And I'm sure the stars will all align for you." I nudge her flamingo raft playfully. Sam gives a small smile and is about to say something when, out of nowhere, we're suddenly *drenched* in water.

"*MARIEEEEEEE!*" I scream, wiping water furiously from my eyes. But when I blink the

chlorinated blur away, I don't see my sister like I thought. Instead, I see two very wet, slobbery furballs just inches from my face.

"Rocket! Cosmo! You little fluff butts!" I shout at them. Sam laughs and splashes the dogs with water, but instead she gets me even wetter, and now *it's on*.

Before we know it, the pool is a massive cyclone of splashing and shrieks, each of us seeing who can douse the other with the biggest wave, forgetting all about school and boys and the stars up in the sky that might or might not be guiding us.

Chapter 3

"You look super cute," I tell Sam as soon as she steps out of her mom's yellow Beetle.

"*You* look super cute!" Sam answers, giving me a hello hug.

Sam's flowy peasant top is working for her, just like it did at our at-home fashion show. Except, this isn't a dress rehearsal. This is our first day at JFK Middle School.

We stand in front of the school building, gawking. Everything is so different from what we're used to.

I nudge Sam with my elbow. "Check it out—the bike rack out front is crowded."

Sam nods. "And look, some kids even skateboard to school," she says.

"Is it me, or is everyone on their phones?" I observe.

Sam's mouth hangs open. "It's like selfie central out here."

Looking around, there are no parents asking their kids to pose for the millionth photo. No tiny

faces beaming up at us with admiration.

"I'm kinda missing the sparkly backpacks," I say.

Sam curls out her bottom lip and frowns in understanding.

It's a good thing Sam and I coordinated our arrival times. I don't feel so alone with her beside me.

"Have a great first day, girls!" a man calls out.

I whip around and notice my parents haven't left yet. My dad's sentimental smile emerges from the passenger side window. *Guess I'm even less alone than I thought.*

"Uh. Thanks, Dad," I say, narrowing my eyes and hoping he gets the hint not to linger.

I'm just glad I got Mom to chill at least. She'd started to get out to take my picture, but I begged her to stay in the car with Dad. Yes, they *both* insisted on dropping me off. And on picking me up later today. *I hope they don't keep this up all week.*

The shrill of the school bell knocks us into action. There's a teacher standing at the front door. Instinctively, Sam and I form a single file line as we make our way to her.

If we want to get to class on time, we need to be as close to first in line. But someone is beating us to the teacher—a speed-walking boy who seems intent on snatching the line leader title. But ha! We're second and third in line.

Sam walks with her head high, giving all the slowpokes a *me-first* look as the teacher holds open the weighty door, gesturing for us to enter. We follow the line leader into a smallish entryway.

Fun fact: The speed-walker is also a loud talker. He turns around and says, "Get off my heels! Why are you following me?" His voice bounces off the walls and rattles my first-day nerves.

"Isn't this the line?" I speak up, even though I'm confused.

"There is no line. *Duh*, this is middle school."

He and a friend who just walked in laugh like evil villains and point their crooked fingers at us.

Cringe!

Sam and I slow down, putting some distance between us and the hecklers. They walk through the double doors and into the school like they own it.

"He's probably some eighth grader who thinks he's boss," Sam assures me when she sees the mortified look on my face.

"You're right. We probably won't bump into him ever."

We step through JFK Middle School's double doors and are hit with a cool blast of air. We stand in awe for a moment.

The high ceiling foyer, the throngs of unfamiliar faces. The lifelike tiger standing in the middle of everything, representing the JFK Tigers. Even more surprising than the giant furry mascot is the type of kids walking around. They're so much bigger. And no exaggeration, we walked past one kid with a . . . mustache?

"I feel like I've just entered another planet," I say.

"Guess that finally makes you a real-life Galaxy Girl." Sam smiles. She looks more excited than nervous. Unlike me.

Our elementary school was pretty small. But this place is big enough to fit three elementary schools—literally.

Off the bat, you can pick out the kids from my old school, Summit Elementary. Like Sam and me, they're walking around like wide-eyed tourists. The two other elementary schools are from the cooler parts of town, where the population is higher and

there's lots of fun stuff to do. Those kids may be new to middle school, but it's not obvious. Aside from just looking smaller, they seem to blend right in.

I walk Sam to her locker, and then she comes over to mine. We plan to walk each other halfway to class, but then the bell rings again. Everyone starts slamming lockers and scattering into classrooms, banging into anything and everything with oversize backpacks.

"We're going to be late for class!" Sam says hurriedly. She looks at her schedule. "I'm this way. Social Studies, room 106D."

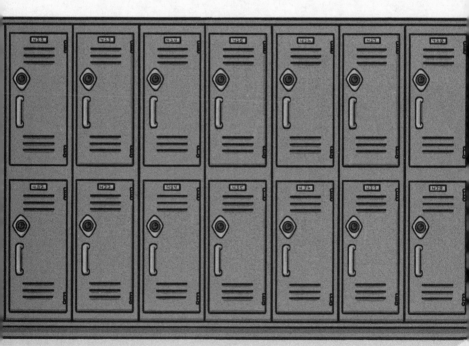

I look at the half slip of paper clutched in my hand and scan frantically for my first-period classroom number. "I have Advanced Science in 304B, which is that way." I point in the opposite direction. I turn to Sam, all at once realizing that this is it—the first time *ever* that Hope Roberts and Samantha Bowers won't be in class together. She squeezes my hand—I hadn't even realized we'd been holding hands.

"Good luck!" she says.

"You, too!" I reply. "Meet me after school? Carpool with me to my house?"

Sam nods and runs down the hall. "You know it!"

And then she's gone.

Chapter 4

I follow the frenzy of students down the hall and somehow cattle-herd into classroom 304B just as the final bell rings. I can sit . . . anywhere? Somehow, most of the back seats are already filled, so the front row it is.

I'm making my way to the empty desks, when I notice the speed-walking heckler from outside. Worse yet, he notices me.

His mouth slides to the side of his face as he leans over and says something about me to his sidekick. They both chuckle obnoxiously.

I guess he isn't an eighth grader. Just my luck.

Trying my best to ignore him, I stare at a NASA

poster on the front wall. It reminds me of my dad. He's got the same one. Something familiar is what I need right now. Nearby to that is a famous photo of Albert Einstein playfully sticking out his tongue, which makes me smile. And ooh! There's a flyer for the after-school science club! *Maybe Sam would want to join, too, so we could spend time together.*

I'm seated next to a girl with long dark hair. She's already pulled out a binder and pencil and looks at full attention. I follow her cue and focus on the adult in the room.

In his crisp white jacket, the teacher looks like an actual scientist. He's writing his name on the board: Mr. Gillespie. When he turns around, his expressionless face is the exact opposite of Einstein's playful tongue-out poster.

"Can anyone tell me why you're here?" Mr. Gillespie asks in a strong voice that startles us all to attention.

Kids exchange uncertain glances before a boy in the front of the classroom raises his hand. "Because we all got the letter?" he asks.

Mr. Gillespie nods but clicks his tongue. "True, you all did get the letter. But no—you are here today because each of you has the potential to be the next great scientist."

Mr. Gillespie points to a boy in the back with curly red hair. "One day, you might cure cancer," he says. He points to a girl in braids at the front. "You might be the first person to land on Mars." And then he looks to me. "And you might change the world."

I feel a rush of pride, excited to hear him tell us

the same thing I say to myself and to anyone who will listen! It's true—we all *can* make a difference. And we can do it today, tomorrow, *and* "one day."

"My job is to give you the tools to do all that," Mr. Gillespie continues. "Starting right now. Please open your textbooks to section thirteen."

Feeling energized, I pull the textbook out from under my desk chair and quickly flip to page thirteen.

"Can anyone please read the first paragraph on Newton's laws of physics?" Mr. Gillespie asks.

I eagerly shoot my hand into the air. Mr. Gillespie points at me and asks me to state my name.

"Hope Roberts," I announce.

"Hope Roberts," he repeats. "Please, go ahead."

I grin and start to read before even looking at what's really on the page. "'The mating habits of fruit flies will be the main subject of this section,'" I read. "'By doing a cross section of the gene pool, our analysis will—' Wait, what?"

Snickers ripple across the classroom, and my cheeks grow hot. I frantically look around at everyone else's books to see what's wrong with mine.

"You're supposed to be on section thirteen," the girl with dark hair next to me whispers. "Not page thirteen."

I realize with a sinking feeling she's right. I turned to the biology section of the textbook, not physics.

The laughter continues, and the same obnoxious speed-walker whispers loudly enough for me to hear, "Are we sure *she* got the letter?"

"All right," Mr. Gillespie says as I sink down into my chair. "This is a good example of one of the main axioms of science: Always pay attention to details. Hope, why don't you turn to section thirteen and try again?"

I sheepishly do as he says and start reading. But I feel deflated, like all the energy has been sucked out of me. I really wish Sam were here. She wouldn't laugh at me.

✎☆❀

I managed to get through the rest of the class without embarrassing myself. When class finally ends, I make my way to second-period Spanish. The classroom happens to be across the hall, so this time I'm able to find a seat without being the last one in. I pull out my binder and begin to write the date at the top of the page when the dark-haired girl from

science class comes in and takes a seat in the front row. Quickly, I gather my things and slide into the seat next to her.

"Hey," I say. "Thanks for helping me out in science. It was really nice of you."

Her smile is mixed in with some sympathy. "No worries." She effortlessly sweeps her long hair back over her shoulder.

"What's your name?" I ask.

"Camila Rose Rivera," she answers proudly.

"That's a cool name," I say. "I'm Hope No-Middle-Name Roberts."

Camila gives another sympathetic smile. "I know your name. You said it to the whole class before."

"Oh yeah," I say sheepishly. "Was my mix-up as bad as it looked?" I'm secretly hoping she'll say it wasn't.

"I bet you no one will remember it in a few weeks," says Camila.

"I know one kid who won't let anyone forget. The boy who joked that I shouldn't be in the advanced class."

"Oh, don't listen to Connor." Camila shrugs as the class starts to fill up around us. "He's always got a chip on his shoulder."

"Connor?" I ask.

"That's the kid who made fun of you. Everyone knows who he is."

She waits for me to say I do, but I shake my head since I clearly don't.

"His mom is a famous neurobiologist," she says. "He's one of the smartest kids here, but he's gotten such an attitude ever since—"

"Bienvenidos," the teacher says, suddenly interrupting all the chatter in the classroom. "My name is Señora Lopez," she says, her hoop earrings swaying with her head movements as she writes her name on the board.

"Well, hopefully I can redeem myself tomorrow, because science is my superpower," I whisper to Camila. "Just like how Spanish is one of your superpowers, right?"

Camila makes a weird face. "Why would it be my superpower?"

"Because, you know," I say, thinking it's obvious. "You're Latinx?"

Camila's expression changes. I hadn't meant to upset her—I swear, I hadn't. But she's clearly not happy with me.

"I mean, um . . . Your name . . . Aren't you from . . . ?" I stutter, embarrassed.

"My grandparents are Guatemalan, if that's what you mean," she says bluntly. I open my mouth to respond, but I can't think of what to say. So instead, I awkwardly turn back in my seat to face the front of the classroom while Señora Lopez continues to write on the whiteboard.

Sixth grade is not off to a good start.

Chapter 5

"**T**ell me everything! I want to know how you spent the day without me!" I beg, then desperately wait for a response.

Cosmo and Rocket both stare blankly at me and then roll over and go back to sleep on the fuzzy white rug they love so much. Sometimes I suspect they come to my bedroom to cuddle with that rug instead of to hang out with me.

"I guess that's my answer." I chuckle to myself. No matter. I'm sure they're dreaming of our summer days spent together. I sit on the floor, rubbing their bellies until Sam races in, breathless.

"Okay, I just had the *most* awkward moment," she

says. She paces back and forth, her arms flailing this way and that. With all my parents' first-day questions (and there were tons of 'em), Sam and I hadn't had the chance to catch up on our car ride home before we dropped her off a few blocks away at her own house.

As strange as it sounds, I'm getting excited by the idea that I'm not the only one who bombed today. Rocket opens one eyelid when, in anticipation of Sam's story, I stopped rubbing her belly.

"What happened?" I ask.

"I ran into Josh—twice!"

I barely raise an eyebrow.

"Burger Boy from camp," she clarifies, her voice higher pitched than usual.

Now I'm curious. "Wait, really?"

"The first time was at school when I saw him hilariously trip over his own feet before fourth period. I LOLed—I couldn't stop myself," Sam says, and then covers her own mouth, trying not to laugh again.

"And the second time?"

"That's the awkward part. It was just now, right outside your house!"

"No way!" I jump up and dash to my bedroom window with Sam on my heels.

"Wait! What are you doing? He'll see us!" Sam tugs on the curtain I'm trying to hold open. I let her win this tug-of-war, but not before I get a glimpse of a lanky boy making his way down my street.

"Skater Boy's name is Josh?" Marie and I call him that because we've never seen him walking. He skateboards everywhere he goes. I guess he's a lot less clumsy on wheels.

Sam's eyes go wide. "Burger Boy is Skater Boy?"

"Look on the bright side," I tease, plopping onto my bed. "Now you know two places to bump into your crush."

Sam free-falls backward next to me. "The problem is, I don't think I want to bump into him anymore."

"Why? If he's as clumsy as you say, it shouldn't be too hard!"

She shakes her head at my cheesy joke but still can't help but giggle. Hearing Sam's hiccupy laugh always gets me going. I crack up, which only intensifies her laughter. She rolls onto her side.

I'm hunched over and can barely catch my breath, but I have another thought.

"Do I need to remind you how messy you are on roller skates?" I chuckle at the memory. "Imagine you both hanging out together—you on wheels and Josh on his feet!"

"You are so silly!"

We laugh so hard that we tumble to the floor. Acting as goofy as we always do when we're together feels good after the day I've had. It's almost like all the embarrassing things that happened to me are fading away. At least for the moment.

"What's so funny?" Marie walks in, phone in hand. She smiles when she sees us both collapsed on the floor. "Sounds like someone had a decent first day of middle school."

"It was . . . interesting," I say, sitting up.

"That's good."

Marie gets a text, and her attention is already gone. She scrolls for a second. "Oh no!"

"What happened?" asks Sam.

"Looks like the Eastern Shore Animal Shelter where

we got Cosmo and Rocket may close down," she says without looking up from her screen. "Not enough funding."

"Oh no," I say, instantly bummed. I look at our dogs lying peacefully and think about all the pets that will miss out on finding a forever family. How could something like this happen? What will happen to the dogs they're caring for right now? *They can't close!* "We have to do something."

"You're going to have your hands full with schoolwork," says Sam. "Besides, Saturn is totally not in the right celestial orbit for resolving a crisis."

Sam looks to Marie to back her up, but Sam's new astrology talk is lost on my sister. She's back to

texting on what seems like another matter entirely.

"I'm sure it'll work out," Marie says, looking at her phone.

In a text trance, Marie walks out of the room, already on to the next thing.

Sam catches the bummed look on my face. "I know what you're thinking: First save the dogs, then save the world."

Busy schedule or not, I can't just turn my back on this or un-hear what Marie said. "Maybe there's some way I can still help."

I glance over at my Galaxy Girl comics and imagine how many people I could help with her superpowers. Or if I had her power to turn back time? I'd for sure go back and fix the embarrassing mistakes I made at school today.

I reach for Mars, a round planet pillow on my bed, and toss it to Sam.

"Okay, spill the tea," I say. "Running into your crush can't be the most awkward moment of your day."

"Believe me, it was." She tosses the cushy planet back to me.

"You're telling me you felt right at home at JFK Middle?" I throw Mars back, a little too hard. Sam catches it like a pro.

"Oh, I had the most epic time!"

"You did?"

"Yup. I even answered some questions in math class when no one else could. It felt good being the smart one for a change."

Advanced-class invitation or no, Sam is one of the smartest people I know. I'm lost in thought about this when the planet careens straight for me, plopping me between the eyes.

"Oops! I'm so sorry!" Sam gasps, though she's smiling.

It's almost like she's apologizing about my sucky day.

"How about you? Did you like your classes?"

"It wasn't anything to talk about," I say, reluctant to give her my gory details now. "Hey, one cool thing is this science club. You want to join together?" I crawl over to my backpack and grab the flyer.

Sam looks apologetic.

"I was hoping to try out for the fall musical with Lacy Torrisi."

"Lacy Torrisi? Mansion-living, personal-butler-having Lacy Torrisi?"

Sam shrugs. "She's actually pretty cool. We have most of our classes together."

"Oh."

"But I promise to come to your science competitions, if you promise to come to my opening night." Sam holds out her palm, and I meet it with mine.

"Deal," I say, forcing out a smile. But inside I'm wondering how it could be that things have changed so much in just one day.

Chapter 6

Everyone makes such a huge deal over the first day of school. What about the second day, when you have to deal with the *fallout* of an embarrassing first day? I slide into my seat in science class, unnoticed. *Whew.* Now, I just have to make it through class—and the next class, and the next class—incident-free.

I unfold my school schedule and examine it. This week is going to drag if I keep stumbling through the most basic interactions with people. I can't be this *Hope*-less without Sam.

Can I?

I can't deny it when I look at the data. After

all, facts never lie. Between the two of us, Sam is the people person. Almost everyone I know, I met through Sam. So to turn things around from here, I need to do what I think Sam would do.

Camila takes the seat next to me.

"Hi, Camila," I say.

"Hi."

While Mr. Gillespie is in the doorway talking to a teacher, chirping breaks out in all corners of the room. Camila and I, though, sit in awkward silence. Now's my chance to make things right.

"I, uh, looked up the origin of my name," I tell Camila. "'Roberts' is from England. But I've never

been there, and neither has my dad." I shrug. "I can't even say I eat English muffins all that often."

Camila looks at me. "So I take it English stuff is not your superpower?"

I smile, relieved she gets where I'm going with this. "Yes. Apparently, there's more than one way to be a Roberts."

Camila shakes her head, but the corner of her mouth curls.

"I'm so sorry I jumped to conclusions about you. All that talk about Spanish superpowers was nothing but super judgy."

"Yes, it was," says Camila.

"And Super Judgy as a comic book character would probably have, like, the weirdest costume."

"It wouldn't be a good look, for sure."

We both snicker.

"Are you ready to learn some science?" Mr. Gillespie is asking the two of us. We hadn't realized the surrounding chatter had stopped.

We nod.

Welp, this class was *almost* incident-free. But I'm okay with that.

✐☆❀

If you could flip through the comic book highlights of my next few days, the action panels would play out like this . . .

Wednesday: A science pop quiz. Panel 1: Me thinking I did great. Panel 2: Me hoping I did great. Panel 3: The bubble above my head reads, *Why is Mr. Gillespie taking so long to grade these quizzes?!*

Thursday: Camila and I eat lunch together. (I bring in English muffins!) I think I've made a new friend.

Friday: It's here! The first day of the after-school science club!

But first, I have to get through the school day. First up, Mr. Gillespie's class. I sit, tapping my feet, watching Mr. Gillespie snake his way around the classroom with a stack of papers, the scent of peppermint candy wafting behind him. It seems like he's handing out the quiz results to everyone but me. *Did he lose mine or something?*

He randomly makes stops at different desks and walks right past mine several times.

Aw, come on!

It's like getting faked out by a waiter carrying a tray full of yummy dishes, while you sit there with your stomach grumbling.

Reactions are erupting in different corners of the room. Some people sit back and sigh in relief. Others hunch their shoulders and flip their papers, facedown. Mr. Gillespie seems to be enjoying this, though you can't tell from the dull expression on his face. His deliveries have a touch of dramatic reveal—an extra snap of the paper, a flip of the wrist, a hand flourish.

"Nice!" exclaims Connor, the annoying boy who embarrassed me the first day. He high-fives his sidekick, Shep. I have to force myself not to roll my eyes.

"Whew!" I hear Camila utter under her breath. I pivot to face her and give her a slight smile when she catches my eye.

When I pivot forward again, my quiz is finally lying on my desk, facedown.

Uh-oh. That can't be good.

I swallow down my panic. My now clammy fingers slowly flip the paper back over.

100 percent!

It feels like I'm holding a brand-new issue of Galaxy Girl right now. I could dance in my seat. I could shout wahoo! I could—

"Miss Roberts, please settle down."

The entire class chuckles.

OMG, OMG, OMG! I didn't even realize I had high-pitched squealed aloud!

"Sorry," I say. I'm grateful the humidity has made my hair a little bigger today. I look down and let the curly strands curtain my face from the stares.

Squeal slip aside, I walk out of class with a bounce in my step. Things are looking up. I aced the quiz, and science club is just a few hours away. Ending this first week of school on a high-pitched note? I got this.

☄☆✾

The science club meets in what looks like a cool robotics lab. There are all sorts of gadgets and equipment on the counters lining the walls. Mr. Gillespie is setting up a screen for a presentation. In the center of the room is a big U-shaped table. There's plenty of space there to tinker and experiment with things up close. Plus, the small bowl of candy at each end looks so inviting.

I see familiar faces around the room—Camila, a quiet girl from my Language Arts class named Grace, Shep . . . and Connor. *Great.*

I take the empty seat between Camila and a boy wearing a basketball jersey. He's just helped himself to two pieces of candy—one he eats and the other he saves in his pencil case. If Sam were here, she'd for sure notice that this boy is kinda cute. But I'm not *noticing.* I'm making an observation.

"Hey," I say to Camila.

"Hey," the boy answers back instead.

"Um, hi," I respond, feeling slightly embarrassed for him.

Camila smiles and gives me a little wave.

"Welcome to the first gathering of the science club!" Mr. Gillespie walks in looking way more animated than he does during the school day.

When he has us each introduce ourselves, I learn that the boy sitting next to me is a seventh grader named Henry Chen. The only other seventh grader here is a kid named Ezra.

"We are gearing up for our first science competition. Some of you have heard it referred to as the 'new-year competition,' for obvious reasons. But I like to call it the three-week dash. In less than a month, we will enter what we do here in the competition. So I hope you've come prepared to innovate," declares Mr. Gillespie, twisting a piece of candy wrapper.

Everyone sits up and nods enthusiastically. I'm clearly not the only one excited to be here. With that, Mr. Gillespie clicks his laptop, and a slideshow pops up on the pull-down screen. There are pictures from last year's science fair and all of the robotic competitions. Supercool projects. A great team. Ezra is in most of the photos. I catch a glimpse of Henry in the background of another picture.

"The idea we enter this time has to follow the theme 'Spectacle,'" explains Mr. Gillespie. "Anyone, tell me what the word 'spectacle' means to you."

Grace raises her hand.

"Chaos," the kid named Ezra shouts.

Grace's mouth parts like she's about to say something.

"Not just chaos," says Connor. "It can be anything over-the-top, but in a good or bad way."

Mr. Gillespie holds up his finger. "Ah, but there's a missing ingredient in these definitions. Know what that is?"

Connor is silent.

"An audience," says Grace.

"Yes! The eyeballs—or the views, as your generation would put it. Over-the-top behavior—good or bad—on display. So. Any ideas what attention-grabbing spectacle we can base our project around?"

Camila is the first to raise her hand.

Mr. Gillespie points at her.

"We could—" she starts.

"How about something with a toy train?" Connor says at the same time, only louder.

"Good call," says Mr. Gillespie. "But we've featured trains too recently."

"We could make a chain reaction," Camila gets out this time. Unfortunately it's the same time Shep says, "Let's do a laser–light show!"

"Too close to what our eighth-grade Advanced Science class is presenting on day two of the competition," says Mr. Gillespie. He then looks to where Camila, Henry, and I are sitting. "But did I hear someone in this area mention a chain reaction?"

"I did," Camila answers timidly, unsure if Mr. Gillespie is for or against her idea. "Chain reactions are popular with science-video viewers, so I thought that would make the perfect spectacle."

"I like that," he says. "Unique, not been done. Let's build on it. What type of chain reaction?"

Mr. Gillespie turns his back to us and starts looking for a working whiteboard marker.

Next to me, Henry has a tiny basketball eraser,

which he's bouncing on his notebook. As soon as he rests his eraser on his notebook, he sneezes and, in doing so, accidentally tips it, causing the eraser to roll down the table to his pencil case. There, it shakes loose the piece of candy he tucked inside, which then slides straight to me.

"Help yourself to a Starburst." Henry gives me a cute—er, nice—smile.

That's when an idea hits me. "We can make it a Rube Goldberg—"

"Mr. Gillespie, you spelled *chin* reaction," Connor interrupts me. He even manages to make his helpfulness sound like taunting. Maybe it's a gift.

"Oops, thank you!" Mr. Gillespie uses the side of his fist to erase his mistake. "I'm trying to write as fast as the thoughts are coming."

Henry leans toward me. "That's a cool idea. But I don't think he heard you."

"Go ahead, Henry," says Mr. Gillespie. "You were saying something we can make?"

Grace and Camila exchange a look across the table. I glance at them both, and the three of us widen our eyes, like, *Seriously?*

"It wasn't me," says Henry.

"It was me," I say.

"*This* ought to be good," says Connor, who's smirking like the prince of snark.

With that remark, it's like Connor's put a spell on me. My tongue feels tied into a knot. All eyes around the table are on me. I actually have everyone's attention, and I'm about to blow it.

Mr. Gillespie sighs. "Settle down, and be respectful when someone has the floor, please." He looks at me. "Miss Roberts?"

I can feel Henry and Camila telepathically urging me to speak up. I catch Grace's eye, and she gives me an encouraging nod.

I try blanking out everyone but Mr. Gillespie. "A chain reaction that's like a robotic Rube Goldberg machine," I say, my voice getting stronger. "Rube Goldberg machines complete a simple task through complicated steps. But we can take it even further by coding custom robotics to get everything started."

"Miss Roberts, I think you've presented our winning competition idea."

A buzz of excitement breaks out. Some people applaud, and others—like Connor, who's already sketching something—get to work right away. I can't stop grinning.

"Awesome!" says Camila.

"It was your idea that kicked things off," I remind her.

Camila smiles. "We started a real-life chain reaction."

"Let's break up into groups," says Mr. Gillespie. "The chain reaction team and the robotics team."

As I sit there waiting to be assigned to a team, I miss out on actually choosing where I want to go. A group of kids—Connor, Shep, Grace, and Ezra—have already walked over to the robotics equipment and have begun sorting through pieces. Somehow, Henry, Camila, and I get saddled with making a chain reaction.

There's an excited buzz swirling Connor, Shep, Grace, and Ezra. And on our side of the room, not so much.

Somehow Connor is looking at us while talking to his new teammates. "This'll be challenging, but we've got the best brainpower on *this* team," he says.

Grace rolls her eyes at Connor and throws an apologetic glance our way. "Can we just get started?" she says.

"Chain reaction team?" Camila whispers to me, annoyed.

I huff. "Let me guess—not your first choice, either?"

The only person happy about this is Henry.

"You guys—I have so many ideas," he says, tossing his tiny basketball from one hand to another.

"Now, for the chain reaction team, don't view yourselves as simple domino handlers," Mr. Gillespie says, looking in our direction. "What you're doing is just as important in a competition that's all about spectacle."

I don't want to make a bigger deal about this than it should be. But still, this project was our idea, so how did Camila and I wind up *here*?

Chapter 7

The three-week dash begins now. We decide that the setting of our project is an amusement park with tiny model roller coasters and everything. (That was Henry's idea.) A robot will be programmed to spark a wacky chain reaction throughout the entire park. We're still planning out how exactly everything will unfold.

It's supercool, and I'm excited about it. I'm just not loving my role in the whole thing. But, who knows? Maybe there'll be another real-life chain reaction where Henry's enthusiasm will rub off on me and Camila.

Before leaving our first science club meeting,

both teams plan a few extra lab meet-ups when we all can keep working together. The next one will be Monday before school.

"Was science club everything you dreamed it would be and more?" Mom asks when I get in her car a few minutes later. She's wearing her huge sunglasses today, so about half her face is hidden.

"Yup," I say, sparing her the awkward details.

"Good." When she smiles, her cheekbones lift her shades way over her eyebrows. "And you've officially completed your first week of middle school! Are you and Sam going to celebrate this milestone?"

I smile back. "I'm not sure yet. I'm waiting for her to answer my text."

Sam can be a little scattered and forgetful, so I give her some time to get back to me. But when I don't hear from her by the time I'm walking into my room, I call her on video chat.

Cosmo and Rocket want my attention just as much as I want Sam's. They're both jumping on my leg, like they want me to carry them. "This is important human stuff, guys," I tell them, kicking off my shoes and taking a seat on my bed. "I've got to tell Sam about the disaster that was science club."

"Hey!" Sam answers after the first ring. She has the phone so close to her face, I can see food crumbs on the corner of her mouth.

I grab the Mars pillow, put it in my lap, and lean my elbows on it.

"Yay! I'm so glad you picked up. I gotta tell you about—"

Howling laughter echoes in the background.

"Are you out somewhere?" It's no use attempting to peek behind Sam. Her face takes up the entire screen, just like my hair takes up mine.

"N-no, I'm home," she says sheepishly. A strip of sunlight appears across Sam's ivory face. She's walked toward a window, away from the noise.

Sam lives at home with her mom. As far as I know, all her cousins live too far away for a pop-in visit. A few more voices ring out at Sam's house.

"Who's that?" I ask, still clueless.

Sam's mouth goes all square-shaped, like she's feeling guilty. "Lacy came over. We're helping each other choose the perfect audition monologue."

"Oh."

"And then some of her friends texted, found out what we were doing, and asked if they could come,

too. Before I knew it, we had an instant audience. And they brought snacks!"

"I can see that," I say, gesturing to the crumbs on her face. She rubs them off with a grin.

"I was totally going to invite you, but you had science club after school. You can come hang out now, though." She sounds apologetic.

I try to wipe off any look of disappointment on my face. "It's totally fine," I say. "You guys have fun."

"Wait! You were starting to tell me something."

A group cackle breaks out. It sounds like an inside joke, and I suddenly feel like I'm standing way on the outside.

"Was I? I already forgot what it was," I fib. "I'll let you get back to your . . . friends."

I hang up before she can say anything else.

Sensing I'm free now, Cosmo and Rocket get back to begging. But instead of jumping on me, they trot across the room and start pawing at my dresser. Those two know exactly what I keep in there.

"Oh, I get it now. You pups don't want me, you want treats!" I smile and shake my head. "I'm glad *some* things haven't changed this week." Once they see me coming, they sit with their tongues hanging out.

"Same ol' greedy goobers," I tease, dropping two bone-shaped snacks at their paws. "Don't ever change."

Thinking back to what Sam said about me *not* being unpredictable, I'm now willing to admit she's partly right. After a week of middle school, I could use a nice break from the unpredictable.

Give me the Galaxy Girl type of predictability any day. Good guys fighting bad guys, a superhero saving the day. Galaxy Girl was the first human born on a spaceship. And after barely surviving a crash landing on a faraway planet, she acquired superpowers from the rare healing plant found there. She wasn't born a superhero. Galaxy Girl was a normal girl who became something more one day.

When is *my* something more?

I thought it was the letter I received from JFK Middle School. Then I thought it was the science club. But now I'm not so sure.

Chapter 8

I report to the science lab thirty-five minutes before the morning bell, still a bit groggy but relieved to find Camila and Grace already there.

"Whose bright idea was it to have an early Monday science club meet-up?" Camila jokes after we greet each other.

"Yeah, and one week out from summer vacation." I rub my eyes and join the both of them at the project table. If it weren't for my dad inviting me to go with him on his early morning dog walk, I'd be even less alert right now.

"But at least we're the first ones here," says Grace. She glances at the closed room door. "Maybe the others will forget."

We all laugh at the hopeful way she said that.

"Aw, Henry's invited, though," says Camila, gesturing to the mini construction zone with a glue stick. "He makes this chain reaction work more fun."

"Yeah, he's cool." I smile, remembering how pumped he was to start constructing the chaotic amusement park scene.

"It's good that we got here earlier than early," says Grace, picking through the robot parts in a shoebox. "It's nice to be able to finish my sentences."

I start piecing together what will be roller-coaster tracks. "Don't get used to it," I tease.

"Yeah, what's up with all the rude interruptions

going on in here?" Camila grimaces.

"I know. Am I that much of a quiet talker?" asks Grace. "I mean, I can hear myself. But can you guys hear me?"

"Loud and clear," I say, and Camila nods.

Grace tries on a different-sounding voice. "How about now?"

"Yup."

She lowers her vocal volume. "How about now?"

We shrug. "Same."

The lab door swings open as if hurricane force winds propelled it. It's Connor, Ezra, and Shep.

Henry straggles in behind them.

We immediately dive into the work, and again I wish I was programming instead of rigging. But *wishing* for something isn't going to change anything. I've got to make it happen. That's when a thought pops to mind.

"There's no reason our chain reaction can't use a robotic touch here and there," I suggest to Camila and Henry.

"It'll take more work," says Henry, unsure.

"It won't be anything too complicated," I assure him. "Maybe automate some function in the roller coaster or the ticket agent," I say. "It could earn us extra competition points."

"We could try," says Camila cautiously, looking at the detailed blueprint she had begun sketching during our first club meeting. Everyone now referred to it like it was a treasure map.

"You want to make it unanimous, Henry?" I ask.

"If you say so." He scratches his head.

I have another idea to share, one that I'm hoping will set off its own chain reaction of positive results. It has to do with helping change the world—our Science Club world. When Grace, Camila, and I leave the lab together, I fill them in.

"It's not right how whatever we say keeps getting ignored in science club. I was thinking maybe I can conduct a kind of social experiment this week to make sure our voices are heard from now on."

Grace raises an eyebrow. "How will you do that?"

"Yeah, are you going to conduct hearing tests on everyone?" Camila jokes.

"I'm still figuring it all out, but I may need you guys to back me up when I do."

"We've got you," Camila says, and Grace agrees. They both nod, curious but satisfied to wait on the details.

I need a couple of days to prepare my experiment, but I can't wait to get started. And I know the perfect testing ground: math class.

✏︎☆❀

"I had to do my science homework at my dad's bakery yesterday. I hope I didn't get icing on it," says Camila. We're heading from Spanish to math class together. We did this yesterday, too.

"I thought you said you weren't helping out this week?"

"Ezra's bar mitzvah is this weekend, and I wanted to watch my dad make the sample cake."

"How did it come out?"

"So tasty."

"No, I meant your homework," I tease.

"Oh!"

We both giggle.

"All done, and all clean."

"Not that I think Mr. Gillespie would mind frosted paper. Judging from the candy bowl he puts out after school and the crinkly wrappers he's always twisting, he must have a serious sweet tooth."

"There must be all kinds of junk food in his desk drawer."

We crack up again.

"Hi, Hope!" Sam says, beaming. She's walking down the hall toward me, flanked by Lacy plus two girls I don't know.

I can tell Sam is happy she's caught me in a good mood. Especially since she has pretty much been ghosting me since our disastrous video chat last Friday. At first, I thought it was because she didn't want to run into Josh again. But now I see the issue is she's surgically attached to her new friends.

We've sent short hello texts here and there, promising to meet up. But there hasn't been a chance to do that, because apparently Sam comes as a package deal now. It's weird. We haven't gone this long without hanging since Sam spent a month last summer visiting her dad in Ohio.

"Hey, Sam." It's so good to see her, but I feel awkward at the same time. I wonder if it's obvious that I'm so, so jealous. Like, right about now, she and I would normally hug. *Why are we just standing here?* "Um, this is Camila."

"Hey," Camila says as she and Sam smile politely at each other.

"Oh, this is Golda and Charlie." Sam remembers

her manners. "And you know Lacy."

"Hi, Hope!" For some reason, Lacy is super excited to see me. "Have you discovered the perfect soap solution for longer-lasting bubbles yet?"

How did she remember that about me? We were in second grade when pop-resistant bubbles became my obsession.

"You have a great memory," I tell her, impressed.

"Are you kidding me? Who could forget your smarts? We already can't wait to see what your team comes up with at the science competition."

"Wow, that's sweet of you. Thank you." How's this

for unpredictable? Lacy isn't the snob I expected her to be. Super Judgy defeated again?

"You should totally hang with us after school one day. You too, Camila!" Lacy's eyebrows go sky-high. "Sam role plays her favorite theater characters. She's an amazing actor. And Charlie knows everything there is to know about music. And pick your worst subject, and Golda here will tutor you out of any corner."

"And Lacy is never going to let you feel bad about yourself, ever," Sam chimes in. "She's like a human energy drink."

I surprise myself by laughing along with Sam's new friends.

The shrill of the school bell breaks up our friendly huddle.

"Good bumping into you guys. Gotta run!" says Lacy.

"Talk to you later?" Sam asks me.

I nod.

"See ya!" I say as Camila and I wave to the others.

"Hey, mind if I walk with you both?" Golda catches up to us.

"That's right, we're in Advanced Math together. I thought you looked familiar," I say.

"I think I got a mood boost just now," says Camila as we walked away. "And just when I needed one— right before math class."

"I know what you mean," Golda agrees, and I laugh.

We take our seats and open our books. It's finally time to execute my experiment. I only hope I don't chicken out. Math class has the same group-work style as science club, so it's my best opportunity to see if this will fly.

It isn't long before I get my chance.

"Does anyone want to guess?" Our teacher Ms. Wiafe is pointing to a long equation she's just written out in neat numbers.

Experiment step one: I raise my hand at the same time as Connor. I try to ignore the voice inside asking, *Please, please pick Connor.* I lower my hand a smidge, ready to chicken out.

"Hope?" Ms. Wiafe sounds surprised to see my hand, so she's not about to pass up this chance at pulling me out of hiding.

Yikes! Okay, I clear my throat and sit up in my chair, because—stalling. Experiment step two: Speak as loudly, steadily, and confidently as I can muster. "The answer is forty-five."

"Correct," says Ms. Wiafe. "Okay, you know the drill. Come on up and show us how you determined that."

I take a deep breath and stand up. The few steps to the white board feel a mile long.

"The variable goes here." I raise my hand, praying no sweat marks are under my arm. I continue speaking about what I'm writing.

"Ms. Wiafe, we can't hear her," says one of Connor's friends sitting in the back.

In that second I think, *Maybe I'm not ready for this experiment.* I'd rather Ms. Wiafe demand I report to the principal's office. Or maybe I can excuse myself, like, *Hold on, I just need to step out for a bit. I'll be right back . . . tomorrow.*

"I hear her just fine." That's Camila's voice. *Thank you, Camila!* I glance at her, and she seems to be saying, *Go, Hope!*

I clear my throat, stand a bit taller, and continue talking through everything.

Once I write out the rest of the work, I turn around to speak to the class. Here's where my third and most important step kicks in: Do not be intimidated.

"I don't see how you got that," says Connor. He's wearing his smirk on one side of his face again.

I clear my throat, sharply. "Well, *Connor*," I begin before talking through my work.

"It doesn't make sense," Shep says. "You missed a whole middle step."

"I don't know what you mean?" says the girl named Becca who sits a row over from me.

I look at Ms. Wiafe, but she seems like she's enjoying the barrage of questions that keep coming. All she's missing is the popcorn.

I clear my throat and say each questioner's name one by one before answering every question. It's textbook classical conditioning, like Pavlov's famous dog experiment where a dog was given a snack every time a bell rang. Eventually, the dog began drooling every time it heard a bell. My throat clearing and name callouts were prompts designed to train them to pay attention.

"Nicely done, Hope," Ms. Wiafe says after I'm finished. "Everyone get that?"

They did. And I hope they got it loud and clear: *Every* voice counts—not just the loud ones.

Chapter 9

There it is: the Rube Goldberg project and robot prototype. It's rough, but the basic elements are in place. Everyone walking into science club looks impressed by how far we got during our meet-ups Monday morning and Wednesday after school.

We had all been working on different sections of either the robot or the chain reactions, and now here—finally—was everything together. We all go right up to the work table like we're in a trance. We don't back away until Mr. Gillespie walks in and shoos us back a few feet.

"With the slightest bump of the table, this thing may crumble, so let's be careful around it," he says.

"Today is all about checking its programming. Actually, to check *all* the programming, because as I understand it, there are now some tech features in the chain reaction display?"

"Yes," I answer confidently, while hoping my ideas weren't too ambitious.

"You sure we can finish this all in two weeks, Mr. G.?" asks Henry.

"That's up to you all. It's going to take some crafty planning to get everything to come together in time. But I'm sure you can do it."

Right now the robot looks like a bunch of wires and stick limbs on tiny wheels. But it should read the signal we'll transmit. At our cue, the robot will pick up an object and place it in a specific place to trigger the whole chain reaction.

Once we switch on RG (that's what we've been calling the robot), it stands by, ready for its first command. We wait for Mr. Gillespie's cue, but he doesn't give one. He just stands there chewing on a piece of chocolate he popped into his mouth.

When no one budges, Connor walks to the laptop and starts typing. *I guess having a famous scientist mom makes him think* he *gets to be in charge.*

"Can we make sure this is recording?" Connor gestures to his friend Shep, even though the filming is no one in particular's job.

Shep swipes open the camera app on his phone and gives a thumbs-up.

Henry and Ezra place small LEGO blocks next to RG. Camila, Grace, and I are left standing there. Awkwardly. *How is this happening again?* Have I forgotten about the experiment I tested this week in math class?

We wait for RG to swivel around and pick up the red LEGO block. It does, and we all cheer. Everyone high-fives one another, and in that moment, we all feel like a team.

As soon as we stop cheering, the block clatters

back to the table. RG doesn't place it down in the area we've programmed it to.

We try again. But this time, when Connor commands RG, it doesn't even pick up the block. Some of the guys stack the pieces up, but RG still misses.

I walk over to the laptop. Connor doesn't make room for me to stand next to him, so I look over his shoulder.

"How about if you try this, or this," I say, pointing to different coding prompts.

Connor either doesn't hear me or pretends not to, because he doesn't make a move. He's hogging the screen.

Time for round two of my experiment. I take a

deep breath, stand up straighter, and clear my throat. "Connor."

He whips his head around, his dark eyebrows slightly raised.

Did I catch him off guard? I guess he legit didn't hear me. "Excuse me, I want to try something."

"Sure, go ahead." He backs away from the screen.

As I key in the programming we've started using for the other robotic elements in the roller coaster and ticket booth agent, Camila and Grace walk over. I give them room to share the screen.

"The competition is two weeks away, and we have to get this right," says Camila.

"We have more programming work than we started out with," says Grace, scrolling through the code on the screen. "So it's going to take a third team

that can spend more time outside of school working only on the robot."

"I can probably do that," I hear myself say, wanting to dig us out of this hole. In the end, we'll see that it was a good idea leveling up the project by adding more tech tricks to it. But until then, I have to do the extra work to prove it.

"You can?" asks Connor.

Oh, now he hears us.

"She can do what?" Mr. Gillespie asks.

I softly nudge Grace, prompting her to repeat herself.

"Take RG ho—" Connor starts to say.

"I was saying someone needs to take RG home to focus on the programming," says Grace.

"And I said I can do that," I add.

"Are you certain you can take this on, Miss Roberts?" asks Mr. Gillespie. "This effort can make or break the science competition."

Of course, I got this. Galaxy Girl would rise to this occasion, so I will, too. I live and breathe to solve problems like this. My dad is a rocket scientist, so it's in my genes.

"I can do it," I say confidently.

"You sure?" Shep looks hopeful.

Connor's face goes from doubtful to impressed. Mr. Gillespie gave me an out, and I didn't take it. He looks like he respects that kind of gumption.

In fact, everyone seems more confident.

Henry smiles at me, and I look away, hoping that no one can make out how happy I am to see that smile.

"I'll do it. It's at least a few days' worth of work, but I can do it."

The room erupts in cheers again. People are

high-fiving and already talking about working on other elements of the competition.

I feel Camila pat me on my back.

"That's awesome, Hope."

Still, I can't help but think—just like with RG's first LEGO pickup attempt—is everyone cheering prematurely? And for that matter, am I

overpromising?

My best hypothesis would be yes.

☆

Chapter 10

Some of the coolest innovations celebrated all over the world were started in a garage. Everything from famous rock bands to popular tech start-ups—garages can be a lucky place. So why am I standing in my home garage feeling zero inspiration right now?

I stare at all the coils, nuts, bolts, and tiny metal panels scattered over the workstation my grandpa built us. Maybe the air in here is rusting out the cogs in my brain. But no. The garage door

is open, letting in some much-needed fresh air and sunlight. I also used my favorite rock to prop open the door leading into the house. Still, no amount of breeze or beams of light is helping me solve this RG problem. Even Rocket looks confused. She's sniffing the mini screwdriver in my hand, probably wondering how many of these gizmos are edible.

After going through another programming fail over the weekend, and again at yesterday's meet-up, I've decided to take RG apart and rebuild it from scratch. At home. So, basically, I'm my own torturer.

"Hey, watch that tail!" I leap over to steady the

wobbling flashlight Rocket's wagging tail almost whacked off the lower shelf. "If anything here breaks or gets lost, you'll set me back big-time."

Clang, wham, thump!

I whip around and see the brown blur that is Cosmo, flee the crime scene and dart into the house. The sample paint cans that were neatly stacked on the small storage bin all got knocked off. *Sigh.* I do my best to place them back the way they were.

There's nineties music blasting from my mom's Bluetooth speaker in the kitchen. But the sound

ringing out from here in the garage is a text alert . . . again. Sam has been reaching out to me more often since Lacy gave her seal of approval.

What are you up to? Want to come over? she texts. *We can make sundaes.*

I smile wider than a kid-show puppet. How can I turn down a chance to finally hang with my best friend over one of our favorite concoctions? It's so fun—and delicious! We usually pile on more than the usual hot fudge and bananas. We're talking every type of cut-up fruit, sprinkles, and crumbled-up cookies you can think of.

All of a sudden, Mom's old-school jams get me fired up. I bust a dance move, waving my arms and dipping my head this way and that. Rocket jumps on me, and I grab her front paws and dance with her. Besides eating, dancing is her favorite thing to do.

"Go, Rocket! Go, Rocket!" I crack up at how much she's enjoying this. She's hopping on her hind legs and looks like she's wearing a smile.

When we first adopted Rocket, we'd thought she'd stay a shy dog forever. *Look at her now.* It makes me sad to think of the rescues that won't have

the chance to be adopted now that Eastern Shore Animal Shelter is closing.

My text alert chimes again, so I take a commercial break from *Dancing with the Paws* and check my phone.

See if Camila can come, too! Lacy and the girls would love to hang with her.

Oh.

It's the package-deal thing again. *Ugh.* Why did I even fall for it?

No longer in a dancing mood, I go back to staring at my laptop, feeling duped.

A few minutes later, Mom walks in with a concerned furrow in her brow. She's talking on the house phone, and Cosmo is trailing behind her.

"So nice to hear you're adjusting well, Sam," she gushes.

Sam? I look up from my laptop in a panic and start shaking my head.

"Okay, well, hold on for just a second, sweetie, while I see if Hope is around," says Mom, who gives me a questioning look.

I take things up a notch and wave my arms no.

Mom bunches up her lips and heaves a sigh of disappointment. "Let me get her to call you back when she's finished her project, okay, hun?" She says goodbye to Sam and ends the call.

"Everything all right, Hope?" Mom asks me

gently. "Why don't you want to talk to Sam?"

"I'm kinda too busy."

"Too busy for one of your guys' sundaes?"

I shoot my mom a questioning look and wonder if she's psychic. That would be a cool superpower.

"I wasn't digging. She volunteered a lot of information about all her topping ideas."

That's no fun. I liked it better when I thought Mom was psychic.

"I'm busy with this project," I say. "The whole science club is depending on me to get this right."

"How's it working out for you?"

I sweep my hand over all the gizmos I have to piece together. "Not great."

Mom steps closer and puts a gentle arm around me. "You've been out here since you got home from school. Anything your dad or I can help with?"

"No." I sigh, defeated. "I need to figure this out on my own."

"Why? Aren't you part of a science *team*? How come you're shouldering all this pressure by yourself?"

"I volunteered, that's why," I say, my fingers steadily trying to rub the frustration lines out my forehead. "We had to split up to work on all the different tech elements we added to the original idea."

Mom points her head to one side. "What's the real story here? What's got you acting like it's Hope Against the World?"

"This is just a bit tougher than I thought it would be, but I'll figure it out," I say, careful not to worry my mom.

"I believe you can. But you shouldn't be afraid to ask for help. You know, when I was a student at JFK Middle, there weren't any girls in the science club at all. I'm proud of you."

"There are definitely more girls than when you were a kid. I just can't say we're listened to as much as we should be."

Mom's back stiffens. "What do you mean by that?"

"It's probably just me being sensitive." I start screwing tiny wheels to RG's chassis.

"I wouldn't discredit your feelings. If you're picking up on something, it's worth examining. Like, for example, do you girls feel heard by the other members?"

I give a high-pitched scoff.

Mom's jaw tightens and her brown skin seems to hint a glowing red. "That bad, huh?"

I nod and shrug my shoulders at the same time.

Mom looks like she's restraining herself from jumping into her car and driving down to the school to hold a girl-power rally. When she speaks again, her voice is an octave lower.

"Let me guess, that's why you volunteered for this big job?" She doesn't wait for me to answer.

"You know what you need? More girls to lend their voices. More boots on the ground. There's power in numbers, you know."

A thought comes to mind that suddenly brightens up my outlook. "Thanks, Mom."

"Anytime." She kisses me on the forehead and heads back inside.

Mom is right. And I just happen to know a group of girls who are power-boosted by one girl in particular.

My first priority is to put this RG back together. But once I do that, I plan to start a real-life chain reaction.

Chapter 11

"**N**eed a hand with that?" Connor asks me.

Finally, someone has noticed that I am struggling to carry both my backpack and this oversize cardboard box with RG inside into the school. And that someone is—*Connor?*

"Yes, yes, that would be great!"

Expressing that much enthusiasm makes the box pitch a bit too far to my left. I pin the top under my chin and stay the course, steady and focused.

"You know what, lending a hand is not enough. I'll give you two hands," he says, clearly proud of himself.

Connor puts down his backpack and interlaces

his fingers, palms out, and stretches them. Then he proceeds to put his hands together and applaud.

What a winner. Why didn't I just let Dad help me carry it in when he offered? *Ugh.*

I ignore Connor and keep trudging down the long hall toward the robotics lab.

What is it with this school and their high quotient of wisecrackers? My elementary school was a much kinder, gentler place.

Something about being super focused must really lighten whatever load you're carrying, because

suddenly the outer end of the box seems to lift into the air.

"Hi, Hope," says a voice close by.

Huh?

That's when I notice Henry has taken hold of the front of the box and is helping me carry it. He's looking right into my eyes from a closer distance than ever before. *Gulp.*

"To the robotics lab, right?" he asks.

"Yes, that's the one. I mean, that's the direction." I can't get any more awkward right now. Henry is, like, facing me and walking backward. Speaking of which—

"Incoming!" I say to warn him.

Someone is tossing a squishy, and it almost lands on Henry's head.

"Whoa," he says when he feels it graze his shoulder before landing on the floor. I step on it as I walk by, and it feels like that time I stepped into Rocket's poop pile by mistake.

"Ew!" I say at the memory I'd promised myself to keep buried.

"Is it my breath?"

"No, no." I snicker at his confusion. "But cut right!

There's a sign-up table in the hallway. Cut right."
He moves to the left. "I mean my right. I mean your
right—"

Thwack.

Henry backed straight onto the table.

"Are you guys going to Fall Formal together?" the
girl seated at the table asks sweetly, pointing to the
sign-up sheet Henry is now sitting on.

Henry's cheeks turn beet red. My tongue feels
like cardboard, so I'm thankful Henry can at least
speak.

"Uh, w-we're not, uh—" he stammers.

"You have time to decide," says the cheery girl.
"Fall Formal isn't for another few weeks. In the
meantime, care to support our fund-raiser by buying
a cupcake or two?"

I wonder how many bake sales it takes to raise
enough money to support Fall Formal. *Or to keep an
animal shelter from shutting down. Hmm . . .*

Three footsteps later, the box and the cupcake
sliding on top of it are finally at the doorway of the
robotics lab.

"Thank you, Henry," I say, grateful. It's tough to
look him in the eye after the dance-date fiasco. He

doesn't seem to have a problem looking into mine, though. *Double gulp!*

"Hey," I say, walking over to the display in an attempt to turn his attention away from me. "The chain reaction looks like it came out great. How late were you guys here working on it?"

"Don't ask," he puffs. "I had my doubts about putting in too many automated features. But I'm proud of it. I hope everyone else is, too."

Henry mainly focused on all the manual elements of the chain reaction. I can tell the fun details he's added on his own—including a gumball pit. It really does look amazing.

"Because you worked so hard on RG, more people were freed up to help me and Camila get this finished."

Now that it's done, the amusement park setting has tiny people, cones of colorful cotton candy, and cute little signs like YOU MUST BE THIS TALL TO GET ON THIS RIDE. *Wow.*

I can tell Henry is pumped about his work. "Oh, and check this out," he says excitedly. He carefully leans forward, reaching over everything to flip on a switch by the wall. The blinking string lights come on, as does the amusement park music.

I can't stop grinning. "Nice!"

I see the spot reserved for the robot. Good ol' RG is supposed to kick it all off by picking up a LEGO block masked as the amusement park entry fee and handing it to the ticket collector.

Henry walks me through the whole wacky chain reaction. Actually, he kinda mimes it, sometimes stretching out his arms over his head, other times crouching Olympic skier–style. He acts out the entire sequence of events like an animated storyteller.

"Here, let me set off the reaction for you to check out," he says.

"Wait!" I hold up a finger. "Let me get my camera."

I grab my phone and hold it like a documentarian, ready for action.

"Be prepared to be amazed," says Henry.

It pretty much goes like this: Once RG hands over the fee, the ticket collector falls back from the weight of the LEGO. He topples the chair behind him, which then hits a red button that sets off the roller coasters. The roller coasters are automated—courtesy of girl STEM stars Camila and yours truly—to barrel through a gate, and that gate splashes into a gumball pit. One of the gumballs—aided by an invisible string—flies out and hits

the ticket collector on the head, prompting him to remember to hand RG his golden entry ticket.

"And that's all there is to it," says Henry, like this was uncomplicated. He smiles at me, waiting for more of my reaction.

I stop recording. "That was amazing!" I'm bouncing on the balls of my feet as if I'm on a diving board.

"All that's missing is RG working right to get this going."

"It's ready," I say, placing RG right before the amusement park's mini ticket agent.

"Great! Everyone's been talking about how they can't wait to watch it in action after school!"

My stomach lurches. Mr. Gillespie scheduled a final run-through of our project. It's all going down today at our last science club meeting before the big competition.

After hours of tinkering in the garage on my own—despite all my dad's offers to help—I finally and literally cracked the code. I tested RG's performance last night, and it worked! But now, I'm not so sure if that successful test was the exception to the norm.

Ugh. Rookie scientist mistake. I should've done at least three tests to see if the results were consistent, but I was so exhausted, I stopped at one. What if RG doesn't work the next time around?

My phone alarm buzzes me back to the moment.

"Thanks so much, Henry! I totally appreciate your help. Gotta run!"

And I do. I run out of the lab, down the hall, past the now crowded bake-sale table, and weave my way around before-class loiterers, slow walkers, and group-selfie takers all the way to Sam's locker.

Success!

"Sam!" I shout, running up behind her as she walks away in the other direction.

"OMG, Hope! I was just thinking about you."

"I wanted to catch you." I speak fast, so she can get to class and I can have enough time to get to mine on the other side of the building. "We're testing out our science project in the lab today after school, and I thought it would be great to have a girl-power crew there to cheer us STEM girls on. Do you think you and your friends can make it?"

"I can for sure, but I'll find out about everyone else and let you know!"

"*Thankyouthankyou!*" I say before zipping off down the hall.

✐☆❀

Later that afternoon, the cafeteria is buzzing with chatter and dizzying activity.

Where could Camila and Grace be?

"Hey!" Camila waves me over to a table by the far side of the cafeteria.

"I think I need noise-canceling headphones," I tell them as I take a seat.

"Here you go." Grace hands me cotton balls I recognize as cotton candy props for our chain reaction display. I crack up and hold them near my ears pretending they work.

"Hmm . . . this is how we must sound to Connor," I joke, and we snicker some more.

"I blame the bake sale fund-raiser for all this noise. It's got everyone thinking about the Fall Formal, who's hanging with who, and who's wearing what to the dance."

Just then my phone buzzes. It's a text from Sam.

The girls will be there, ready to cheer you on!

"Perfect!"

"Oh, no." Camila looks like she's got a tummy ache. "Are you excited about Fall Formal, too?" she asks. "Because I'm too tired to pretend I am."

"No, it's not that. And why are you so tired?"

"We were working so late on the amusement park. I was starting to regret not helping you with RG."

"The display looks awesome! I just saw it."

"I wanted to pull my hair out," says Camila.

"Not that anyone would notice any missing," I tease.

"Add that to the list of things no one in that science club would notice about us," Grace says, shaking her head.

"If that Connor pretends not to hear me one more time . . ." I roll my eyes.

"Grrr," Camila growls, her eyes all squinty.

"I bet you they won't ignore us today," I say, unzipping my lunch bag. "I have a little something up my sleeve," I say mysteriously before taking a big bite of my PB&J sandwich.

"Tell us!" Camila leans forward.

"Are you going to add more tech to the amusement park?" asks Grace.

I smile pointing to my full mouth and shrugging.

"Grrr!" Camila growls again, but this time I'm the prey! I make my bottom lip tremble and cower in pretend fear, which only cracks them both up. I can imagine how goofy I must look, so I can't help but laugh, too.

Chapter 12

It's time for our science club presentation, and Sam and her friends aren't here. I was expecting them five minutes ago, and nothing.

I text Sam a reminder. She doesn't text back.

Guess I better get started. Everyone will be here in less than ten minutes, and I don't want to be caught being anything but ready.

I grab the small, flat shopping bag from my backpack. All the mini doll accessories Mom stored in the basement are here. I inspect the tiny hair bands, the fancy hats, the plain yellow dress, the pink superhero cape. RG is not a Barbie, so I know the dress won't fit. But if I throw on a bow and the cape, the robot will look like a STEM-girl-power mascot. That's *exactly* what I want. I know no one will object to this, because last year's science club dressed up their robot like a superhero, too. Just not a *girl* superhero.

I'm stuffing the leftover costumes back into my bag when Camila arrives.

"RG looks like she's ready for action," she says.

I give her a knowing smile, and she smiles back. Henry and Grace compliment RG's style, too, when they walk in a few seconds later. But I hold my breath when Mr. Gillespie walks in and does a double take at our shared robot.

"I see RG is dressed for the occasion," he says evenly.

"It's a big day," says Camila. *Thank goodness for Camila.*

"I hope you don't mind," I say to Mr. Gillespie, matching Camila's confident tone. "I invited a small audience to watch today, because what's a spectacle without an audience? They're on their way."

"Quite right. It's like a tree falling in an empty forest," jokes Mr. Gillespie. "I see Connor seems to agree that an audience is needed."

What?

Connor walks in with an entourage. He's trailed by four friends I recognize from different classes I'm in.

"It was actually Hope's idea," says Connor. Maybe for the first time in his life, he's all too happy to point out his idea isn't an original one. "I overheard her friend inviting people to science club, and I thought I should do the same."

Sam.

She obviously worked to get kids here, but she didn't think it was important to show up herself?

Mr. Gillespie looks at the clockface hanging on the wall and gestures for Ezra to shut the lab door. The final click of door seals it for me. Sam and her friends aren't coming.

"Thank you, Ezra. Shall we get things underway, everyone?"

We form a crowd around our project.

"Here we are, one week before our big day. This competition is a challenging one precisely because of the short amount of time clubs have to prepare for it." Mr. Gillespie stands before the competition display. He turns around and gives RG and the amusement park a nod of approval. "By the looks of this, I'd say you did a fine job. So let's see it in action!"

We all cheer for our hard work. The guests politely applaud as well. Henry whoops and puts on the lights and amusement park music, and a few people clap with anticipation.

"Hold all celebrations for the end of this trial run," Mr. Gillespie advises with a smirk. "Camera?"

Shep runs over and props up his phone so the camera is pointing squarely on the project. When it's ready, he gives his usual thumbs-up.

Connor doesn't walk over to the laptop for once. I'm the main programmer, so I have the floor.

There's no way I can stall. I guess my best friend is a no-show. But maybe this isn't the worst outcome. Success in front of Connor and his friends could be sweeter than I imagined.

Connor shifts his weight from one foot to the other.

He and his friends are whispering and pointing at RG's costume. I can't tell if they're rooting for RG—*and me*—to succeed or fail.

Here goes.

I sync RG with the software on my laptop, and it responds right away.

Everyone puffs out a collective sigh of relief. It's working! *I did it!*

I use arrow keys to direct RG's movements. Forward to pick up the LEGO ticket. I overshoot it a tad, so I command the robot to back up, which it does seamlessly. The room is as quiet as a snowy day.

RG bends over to pick up the LEGO, which it does with ease. Almost there. Just one last step—RG has to hand the LEGO to the ticket collector. The LEGO is steady and firmly held. There's no chance of it slipping out of RG's mechanic grasp. Just a simple forward movement will bring this home.

I hit the arrow key to command RG forward, but RG doesn't budge. No one seems to notice that the robot ignored a command. I press it again. And again.

A few people glance at me, like they're wondering

why I've paused from my duties.

I swallow hard. My breathing quickens, but I don't give away that my panic is building.

One final click brings RG back to life, but I'd hit the back arrow in my desperation to fix the problem. RG lurches backward, catching the pink cape in its wheels. When RG finally answers the command to move forward, the cape gets sucked into its wheels and RG takes a fast-forward nosedive into the ticketing booth display.

I gasp. We all gasp.

The chain reaction that follows isn't at all like the one we planned. As if having a delayed reaction to

my every unanswered strike of the arrow key, RG is stuck in fast-forward, bulldozing the knocked-down ticketing booth straight into the roller coaster, which destroys the entire structure we spent the last two weeks building. Along the way, the roller-coaster command button gets pinned down and the roller coaster obeys the signal—*of course*—and barrels down what's left of the track. The train crashes with a crack right onto the floor, breaking apart the seats and sending tiny LEGO people everywhere. The string lights lasso everything that hasn't already crashed to the floor in pieces.

"NO!"

There are robot parts tumbling off the table, and the once-impressive amusement park scene looks like it's been hit by a category 5 storm. Wiped out.

Talk about a spectacle—this is a real-life one.

"Is that supposed to happen?" one of Connor's friends asks.

"Seriously, Hope?" Connor can't help but be the first to point the finger at me.

"I—I—"

Poor Henry. He's chewing on his bottom lip and rubbing the back of his neck in anguish as he surveys the damage up close. Grace seems frustrated. Her arms are crossed and she and Camila are all-around bummed.

I'm thinking of running straight home—through the bushes and everything. *I wonder if my clothes are durable enough to keep those spindly branches from scraping my skin.*

In the midst of all this, the lab door opens. "Here's the lab!" Sam calls out.

She and Lacy waltz in like

they aren't late. Why did they even bother coming?

They stop in their tracks when, judging by the tension in the air, they realize they've just walked into something heavy.

"Are we too late?" Sam breaks the silence in the room.

Connor ignores Sam's question, and this is the first time I'm grateful he's back to his rude habit.

He shakes his head. "This is not good."

"Back to square one, kids," Mr. Gillespie says solemnly.

"We won't have time to start all over," says Connor. And he's not just being dramatic.

"My best advice to you is to regroup as soon as possible," says Mr. Gillespie with a tinge of sincerity to his voice. He's trying not to show it, but he feels bad for us. For me, even.

"Come up with a strategy to salvage things, or start on a new project. Either way, I'll expect you to present *something* at the competition. JFK Middle has been a presence there for the better half of the last three decades."

Leave it to me to cut down a legacy in its tracks.

Connor unloads on me. "You hear that, Hope? This time step aside and let people with half a brain come up with the strategy."

"Now, Connor—" says Mr. Gillespie.

"I'm so sick of your attitude, Connor!" I bark. "Just because your mom is a famous scientist doesn't mean you get to walk around like you own this school."

With the mention of his mother, Connor's face drops. He looks wounded and at a loss for words at

the same time. His milky skin now flushed red, he grabs his bag and quietly exits the robotics lab.

Mr. Gillespie looks at me, and then walks out after Connor.

"Geez, Hope, that was harsh," says Henry. "Everybody knows Connor's mom left his dad for another scientist last year. She's never been back for Connor, and he hasn't been the same since."

"I—I didn't know," I say.

This is worse than ruining the project.

This is worse than the first day of school.

It may be the worst day of my life.

Chapter 13

Rrring!

R I raise my head off my bedroom desk and send Sam's call to voice mail for the third time. Can't she take a hint?

Cosmo whimpers judgmentally, as if he knows I'm

ghosting my best friend, and he does not approve. Rocket, on the other hand, seems totally cool with it. If she were a cat, she'd be purring right now. She's blissfully curled up around the base of my chair.

"It's complicated," I explain to Cosmo. "It's not Sam's fault, but I can't help but feel annoyed with her right now."

Again, I rest my head on my desk. My head feels like it weighs a ton.

"That face is too pretty, and that brain too valuable, to burrow like an ostrich." I lift my eyes from the crook of my arms like an alligator peering from the water. Dad comes into view—his tall, lean frame is in my doorway.

"Ostriches don't really burrow their heads, you know," I say in a sad little voice. "That's a misconception."

He smirks. "Fine. You're not pulling an ostrich then. But you're not pulling a Hope, either. Not the Hope I know, love, and admire."

Dad's a clever guy outside of

NASA's walls, too. Case in point—he got me to talk to someone not named Cosmo or Rocket. He knew I wouldn't be able to resist correcting him about the ostrich comment. Busting science myths is kind of like my thing.

But now that Dad has an opening, he won't stop trying to convince me that it's time to feel better. There's no use resisting him. I sit up and walk over to sit on my bed.

"What happened?" He walks in slowly and takes my spot on the desk chair.

I grab my Mars pillow, hug it close, and think for a moment. *How shall I put this?*

"I ruined everything," I begin, tears already welling up in my eyes. "The whole science club has no chance at winning the competition next week because of me. I pretty much put the robot on a collision course in our last science club meeting before the competition."

Dad rubs his chin, the way he does when he's trying to mentally untie a strong knot. Project after project, experiment after experiment, my dad has been on such an amazing success streak. He works hard and smart.

I thought I was doing everything right to be a success, too. I saw myself as capable of following in his footsteps. *Boy, was I wrong.*

"Is there anything you can do to fix it before then?" he asks.

I shake my head, the tears now flowing down my cheeks. Dad moves over to the bed and puts a comforting arm around me. Cosmo jumps into my lap, and I put aside the planet pillow to make room for him.

"It's all on camera." I gesture to my phone sitting

on the desk. I don't know why I spent the last few minutes reviewing the embarrassing scene over and over again. Maybe I really am my own torturer.

Thankfully, Dad's not asking to watch the drama, nor is he picking up the phone to check it out himself. "So how did it all go so wrong?"

I tearfully tell him about everything that happened, sparing no detail so he can get the full, miserable picture. I also tell him about Connor and his boys.

"Well," Dad says with a sigh. "It sounds like you weren't being true to yourself."

"What do you mean?" I ask, searching his hazel eyes.

Dad softly rests his chin on the top of my head. "What was your end goal in all this hard work?"

"For the science competition project to be a success," I say.

He pulls back to look at me. "Bingo," says Dad. "But instead, you got caught up in proving the boys wrong."

"But they *were* wrong," I say, suddenly clear-eyed. My tears have dried up. "Even Mom said so."

Dad's warm smile lights up his face. "Your mother is one of the most passionate, strong-willed people I know. That's why I fell in love with her. But with great power comes . . ."

"Great responsibility," I finish the famous message in the Spider-Man story. "I know, Dad. But I'm not a superhero." I learned that the hard way.

"There are lots of different superpowers." My dad pivots to face me and rests his right foot on his left thigh. I shift toward him as well. Cosmo keeps an eye on me, probably for fear I'll stop petting him.

"Science is one of yours," continues Dad. "And your voice is another. But did you know? There are more ways to use your voice than just speaking."

At some point, Dad's message stops sounding like hollow words and starts feeling like advice I can get behind. Hearing all this, I slowly come to an understanding.

"So instead of worrying about proving the boys wrong, I should have . . ."

"*Shown* them they were wrong by doing what you're good at . . ." my dad hints.

"Which was the science project," I finish. "But I put more focus on trying to prove *my* point than making sure the project was done right."

I think about how I volunteered to fix RG all by myself. Having at least one other person working with me could've made all the difference.

"Your impulse to stand up for what you believe in was good," says Dad.

"I just can't let proving other people wrong be the number-one reason for my choices." I puff out a sigh. "Well, it's too late now. The project is ruined. All we have are videos of our test trials."

Dad nods. "The best heroes learn from their mistakes. I'm sure you'll have a chance to use your superpowers for good again soon." He kisses me on

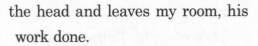

the head and leaves my room, his work done.

"Learn from our mistakes," I echo. I get up and grab my phone from across the room. I think about the mistakes I've made so far this year at school. My error in science class. Jumping to conclusions about Camila's background. Shutting out Sam, even after she kept inviting me to hang out. And now the science project.

One thing is suddenly clear. I owe a lot of people apologies—starting with Sam. She needs to know that I'm not upset at her. Well, maybe a little annoyed that she hasn't made time for just the two of us, but I'm working through that. Besides, I realize I've been busy making new friends, too.

Everything is still pretty messed up. But I can learn from my mistakes to become a better person—and the scientist I want to be.

I gasp, suddenly inspired. An imaginary, floating light bulb pops on above my big hair. Maybe there's no need to hide the mess I've made after all . . .

☆☆❀

It's a half hour before the first bell on Monday morning. I take a deep breath before I reach out for the doorknob, turn it, and push the door open.

Inside the robotics lab is the disastrous project I'm not sure *I* can handle seeing again, along with all the members of science club who I'm not sure want to see *me* again.

Both the project and everybody's hopes seem like they're in a million pieces. That's a whole lot of puzzle pieces to put together, but I've got to try.

Henry is standing the closest to the disaster zone, his arms crossed in front of his basketball jersey. Connor is here. But he's the farthest away from everyone, sitting on a tabletop at the back of the lab. Camila is seated at her usual seat, looking lost. Grace is standing next to the windows, staring outside.

"Thanks for—" I croak like a bullfrog. I clear my throat and start again. "Thanks for agreeing to come here this morning. I'm here to say sorry for not being the team player that I should have been. But I'm also here because I want to turn things around for us. I have an idea I'd like to present that could help us do that. But I understand if you'd rather not go with it."

"We were just sitting here talking about our lack of ideas," says Ezra. "So it wouldn't hurt to hear yours."

Connor heaves out a sigh, and the table creaks as he pivots, but he doesn't leave or say anything in protest.

I give them the details of the plan I've been mulling over. They listen, and it feels good to be

heard. Camila and Grace build on the idea together. Camila is at the whiteboard jotting down all the suggestions everyone has as we brainstorm together. Henry gets to work as we speak, already inspired to start creating the things we'll need.

"It'll take all of us pitching in to get it done on time," says Grace.

"So let's do this," says Shep.

Chapter 14

Here we are. The science competition is finally
here. I stare at the university campus banquet
hall in awe.

The larger-than-life Central Florida Science
Competition banner hangs proudly overhead. It's
royal blue with silver lettering and swaying gently
in the gusts of AC steadily blowing inside. Today is
a sunny eighty degrees, yet goose bumps are poking
through my arms. But uncomfy temps are the least
of my worries.

I'm pretty sure people around me can hear
my heart pounding. Far be it from me to indulge
in science myths, but how could they not? It's

thrumming louder than the music blasting from the homemade paper-and-magnet speakers I'm currently admiring.

It's not just this science project that's this cool. It's all of them. This grand room is full of the type of innovation Mr. Gillespie talked about seeing from us. It's thrilling just being in here. But I can't appreciate any of it if I can't get my mind off what I've done.

Just when I'm finally starting to get over the disaster that was the run-through fail, now I'm nervous about our team's fix for that fail. My dad drove Henry, Camila, and me here an hour early. As planned, we set up our display before the school bus drove Mr. Gillespie and the rest of the club kids here. The science club wanted to surprise Mr. Gillespie. We're hoping he approves of our new presentation.

I thought taking a walk around this room and getting inspired by all the other amazing projects would clear my head and calm me down, but it hasn't helped much. I wish Dad had been able to stay, but Friday afternoons are usually busy for him. He and Mom will be back once the judging is underway. Marie is coming here right after school, but she's got to travel from the other side of town. So for now, I'm on my own.

I make a right at a booth decorated like the interior of a space shuttle and head back to JFK Middle School's science club display. We're located in a busy part of this STEM strip. Our steady competition rankings over the years earned us this prime space.

And lucky me, there's Mr. Gillespie.

Just as I suspected, he has planted himself right in front of the booth with the candy fountain display, his back rigid and his hands clasped behind him. I'm pretty sure it's not because of his keen interest in the physics behind how solid matter can behave like liquids.

That means the school bus from JFK Middle has arrived with the rest of the science club. They'll be surprised to see that our project measures up okay next to everything here.

Maybe I can walk by him unnoticed and slip back to our booth to spruce up our display a little more . . .

"Miss Roberts," Mr. Gillespie bellows, his eyes still glued to the confectionary flow.

Busted.

My words spill out faster than the sugary waterfall. "Oh, I didn't mean to, uh— I just didn't want to disturb you, but I'm totally not avoiding you."

Mr. Gillespie steps away from the booth and faces me. "Are you finished?" he asks, patiently waiting for me to stop tripping over myself.

I nod wordlessly. Mr. Gillespie gestures for us to head over together.

"It's a clever move, the work you've all presented here," he says.

My eyebrows lift. "You've seen it?"

He nods. "Nice work. The mark of budding scientists."

"Thank you. And thank you for pushing us to keep trying," I say sincerely. "We all worked hard on it together."

"What the judges think of this remains to be seen. I've asked the others to take a look around and then meet back up for a discussion. Why don't you man the booth in the meantime," Mr. Gillespie says before he heads off into the crowd.

We're only a few paces away from our space now. There's already a few people checking out our project. Four girls. As we get closer, I can't believe who it is.

"Sam?" I call out.

She turns around and runs up to give me a big hug, even though Lacy and her crew are watching. I hug her back, tight.

Ten minutes ago, I couldn't imagine feeling this ready and confident. "Thanks for being here," I tell her when we pull away.

Sam playfully pokes me in the rib. "Hey, we made a deal. I come to your competitions, and you show up to my opening night."

"You got cast in the fall musical?" I ask, excited and happily caught off guard.

"Yes! Lacy did, too!"

We laugh with relief and high-five each other.

"Hi, guys!" I walk over to Lacy, Golda, and Charlie. "Thanks so much for coming!"

"We wouldn't miss it," says Lacy in her cheerfully encouraging way. I smile, grateful to have supportive people around, because there's no knowing how everyone else will react to the project we're presenting.

"Oh, wow!"

This geeking-out moment is coming from Grace. She's got her phone out, filming all the projects as she approaches our booth. Camila and Henry are right behind her, and Connor, Shep, and Ezra arrive from the opposite direction.

They all have big smiles on their faces when they see the JFK Middle science club sign at booth 1209 and our final project on display.

"Wow!" Shep shouts.

"We did this—?" asks Grace, in disbelief, staring at the display.

The amusement park replica is still in shambles.

RG is still in pieces. But there's a photo of them in happier times, as well as two videos playing on a loop. One video is of the flawless chain reaction I'd filmed that day Henry first showed it to me. The other video is of that disastrous trial run. And the poster above that reads, A STUDY IN SCIENTIFIC AMBITION: LEARNING FROM THE MISTAKES OF A SUPER PROJECT GONE WRONG.

The whole display invites visitors to our booth to acknowledge that failure is a key ingredient in success. Great scientists make mistakes all the time, and that's how they learn and grow.

Grace walks up beside me, staring at the trifold poster detailing our project goals versus our results. "It really did turn out great," she says. "Flaws and all."

"Yeah, I can't believe we pulled it off," adds Henry, as he makes his way around the booth, documenting everything on his phone.

Camila points out a part of what's posted on the trifold poster. "The original blueprint sketches look great here," she says. "Thanks for including them in the presentation."

I smile. "You had such detailed notes, so we had to show that off."

Ezra is pointing at different areas of the display and talking a mile a minute to Shep. Shep smiles and gives me a head nod when we catch each other's eyes. He and Ezra seem pretty pumped about how our booth is set up and making a statement.

We've even attracted a few non–JFK Middle School attendees, who are enthusiastically watching the video. One of them is carrying a clipboard and taking notes. Clearly a contest judge. Sam and I exchange a look of nervous excitement across the room.

The visitors start posing questions to different members of our team. Pretty soon, Grace, Camila, Henry, Ezra, and Shep are guiding mini tours around the booth.

"It took guts to present this the way you did," I hear the woman with the clipboard say to Mr. Gillespie.

"It was their idea to begin with, and they really rallied together and came through in the end," Mr. Gillespie replies proudly.

I guess he approves after all.

Once Connor has finished answering another visitor's question, I walk over to him. He's not acting his usual snarky self. He's still sporting one of his math-riddle graphic tees. But his trademark smirk is replaced with a content nonfrown. This is the first time I'm having a one-on-one conversation with him. As I walk over, I can almost see the chip on his shoulder appear. Having your personal heartache publicly dragged isn't fighting fair, and for that I need to apologize.

I sigh. *Might as well just come out with it.*

"Hey, Connor," I start. "Listen, I'm sorry for bringing up your mom. I had no idea what you've been going through."

Clearly, this is the last topic Connor wants to talk about. He shakes his head, like *Please stop.*

He looks at his feet, all mopey. But then he lifts his chin and recovers some of that stubborn pride he's famous for. "It's okay," he says, his jaw clenching.

"I don't agree," I say loud enough for only the two of us to hear. "A lot hasn't been okay between us. And I'll never apologize for speaking up for myself. But when I make a mistake, I own it. So I'm sorry for jumping to conclusions about you."

In the silence that follows, Connor doesn't follow up with an apology for his rudeness. I kind of don't expect him to.

"It was nice seeing all this set up," he says, gesturing to our booth. "Pretty cool."

"Yeah." I guess that's a step in a healthier direction. And I guess that's where things will stand for now.

"You must be Hope Roberts," the judge with the clipboard says as she approaches me with her hand extended. "You've given us all a lot to think about, young lady. We hope that every entrant who visits this booth grasps its message. It's a strong reminder to us all," she says, giving me a firm handshake.

"JFK Middle does it again," says the man waiting behind her to shake my hand. The lanyard around his neck identifies him as a competition organizer.

I glance over at Sam to give her a thumbs-up, when I notice Marie and my parents watching from the opposite end of the booth, beaming with pride.

An hour later, a large crowd is watching as *we*, the JFK Middle School science club, begin walking up onstage to collect an honorable mention ribbon!

We follow Mr. Gillespie up the stairs with our jaws hanging. *Can this be really happening?* It's the biggest relief to know we can come back next year with our strong reputation intact. You can also hear that relief in Mr. Gillespie's voice as he thanks the judges . . . before passing *me* the mic.

Huh?

"Hope," says Mr. Gillespie. "The team chose you to speak on their behalf."

I stare wide-eyed at my club mates, trying to figure out when this vote took place. Grateful, I accept the mic and say what pops into mind.

"We love science and technology," I say nervously. I hear my own voice projected by the speakers and echoing through the banquet hall, and I see my family watching me from the crowd. My dad catches my eye and winks. Seeing Dad reminds me: *I've got this.*

I clear my throat and continue, and this time the shakiness is gone. "But even though we love STEM, we're still discovering the power of our voices. We have to be brave enough to let this power shine through, and supportive enough to help others shine." I pause and flash a quick grin at Camila and Grace, and they give me a matching thumbs-up.

"If we all keep doing this, innovations will thrive

and bring positive changes to the whole world. Thank you."

Everyone claps and cheers, and I'm so proud I feel like Galaxy Girl saving her planet from evil forces. But it's even better, because this isn't science fiction. This time, it's real life.

Chapter 15

"**R**ocket, be nice!" I scold my moody dog.

I thought she'd be happy to be going on a long walk. When Sam and I made plans to meet up, her mom offered to drive us to our favorite park near the beach. I thought it was the best idea. It's close enough to hear that wave-crashing white noise and breathe in sea-salty air. But thankfully, it's far enough to avoid getting pesky beach sand everywhere and in everything.

"It's okay. She can keep ignoring me," says Sam, holding on to Cosmo's leash. "I just won't give her the snacks in my back pocket."

Cosmo does a double take when he hears the

word "snacks," but Rocket is not impressed. Her leash tightens around my hand as she trots a few paces, showing Sam the back of her head. With that surprise tug, I almost drop my ice-cream cone. (Of course we had to visit the pier ice-cream shop at the start of our walk.)

"Playing keep-away with her snacks is the reason she became your sworn frenemy in the first place," I remind Sam.

"Honestly, I thought Rocket's shade would balance out this sunny day, but she shades so hard." Sam grins, shaking her head.

Rocket throws back what looks to be an eye roll at Sam. That's all it takes. Sam and I lose it. Sam spits out some of the ice cream she's just licked from her cone.

"Rocket, you should've given me a warning before doing that. I would've held off on getting this ice cream!"

Sam's mom is catching up on her reading at the other end of the pier while she waits for us. We enter the dog run, let the pups loose, and take a seat at the last available bench.

I toss what's left of my ice-cream cone in the

trash. Sam still has a bit to go before she's done. We hadn't realized how much the dogs were breaking the ice between us. Now that it's just the two of us, it feels kind of awkward.

"Boy, I can't believe how long it's been since we've hung out alone," Sam says, and I'm glad she's brought it up.

"Well, you've been busy with your new friends," I say, hoping I don't sound too bitter.

Sam looks down at her half-eaten cone and the tiny bit of ice cream left in it. "I'm so, so sorry for getting to the science lab so late that day. After you asked me to come support you! I can't tell you how

bad I felt when I saw your face. I know I let you down, and I want you to know—Huh?"

She's talking so fast, she doesn't realize how many times I've tried to stop her.

"I'm just trying to tell you that *I'm* the one who should be apologizing. What happened that day is zero percent your fault."

I pause for a minute as I watch my dogs crisscross the grassy field together in a blur of black and brown.

"I'm sorry for being distant, Sam," I finally say. "I admit, I was a little jealous." I tug at the frayed hemline of my denim skirt. "You deserve all the friends in the world. I hope that I'm still one of them, despite the Rocket-level shade I've been throwing you."

"Of course you are." Sam loops an arm around my shoulder and squeezes. "I know it must feel like so much has changed, but you're still my best friend. No matter what."

I didn't realize how much I had needed to hear that until that moment. The ocean breeze whips through and carries away any leftover doubts I had about our friendship. I feel so much better.

Sam looks happier, too. But courtesy of the wind gusts, her hair is wrapped around her chin like a beard. We laugh as she tries to untangle herself.

"Oh my gosh, I have so much to tell you!" she squeals. And we start on a long-overdue catch-up.

Sam is acing her classes, and she's even starting

to love her math class. Plus, she has some big news:

"I kind of, sort of, like this boy." She winces and smiles at the same time. "And I think he kind of likes me! Oh, and best of all, our astrological signs are a perfect match!"

Same ol' Sam. I chuckle. "It isn't Burger Boy?"

She swats at the air. "Burger Boy is so last summer. No, but I think he's friends with that kid Henry from your science club."

I feel the corners of my mouth curling up. It's too late to hide it—Sam's quick to notice things like this.

"Hmm . . . ," she says, smirking. "Do you think maybe you and Henry would make a cute superhero couple one day?"

"Maybe you can tell me at your next astrology hangout," I say.

"I will." Sam smiles from ear to ear. "And hey, maybe we can stargaze while you point out each zodiac constellation in the sky."

"Sounds like fun." I grin.

The wind kicks up again.

"Let's go get the dogs. I think it's about to storm," I say.

Sam reaches for her back pocket and pulls out a sandwich bag of dog snacks. Cosmo runs over right away, but Rocket comes to me.

"I don't have any, buddy," I say.

Sam dangles the snack high in the air, the way she used to do to tease Rocket. But then, maybe thinking of all the relationship mending we've had today, Sam has a sudden change of heart. She lowers her hand and holds it out to Rocket.

"Rocket, I want to apologize for withholding snacks just for laughs," Sam says earnestly.

After a moment watching Sam, Rocket slowly and cautiously walks over to her. Unsure, she sniffs Sam's open hand and then pulls back to eye my best friend again.

"It's all yours," promises Sam. "I won't fake you out this time, or ever again."

With that assurance, Rocket's tongue laps up the treat, which she chews graciously. After she's done, she even lets Sam pet her.

"Today's a great day!" shouts Sam, ecstatic and kneeling next to Rocket.

And then abruptly, the sky opens up and the rain comes pelting down.

"Yeah, a great day for a run!" I clip on the dogs' leashes, and we take off sprinting back to meet Sam's mom.

Chapter 16

ow whenever I make a video journal, Cosmo
and Rocket face the screen rather than
face me.

"Am I going to have to get you both Hollywood
agents?" I ask them. I can't even imagine what type
of treats they'd get used to as superstars.

"So," I say to the camera. "I'm not new to middle school anymore. My science project is completed. I learned how to stand up for myself and my ideas while being a team player. But somehow I'm feeling like this is just the beginning for me. Just like I said in my speech at the science competition, I want to use my voice to help others. And I want you— whoever is watching in the future—to be there when I announce this to my parents. Let's go!"

It's movie night, and everyone is in the family room watching TV. They can hear me heading down the hall before they can see me.

"Finally," says Marie.

Cosmo and Rocket run ahead and gather at everyone's feet. Mom isn't big on pets lounging on furniture, and they know it.

"No, just in time!" corrects Dad with a chuckle.

I walk into the family room, my camera pointing at the scene before me.

"There's our baby girl," says Mom. She pats the empty spot on the couch next to her. "We were just about to vote on a movie."

"Oh no, she's filming us for her video diary again." Marie covers her face with her phone.

"This will only take a second," I promise everyone. I set the phone on the coffee table and take my place next to Mom. Now the recording shows everyone: the four of us, plus Cosmo and Rocket.

"Over the last few weeks, I've realized that the things we care about are worth fighting for. And ever since Marie told me about the trouble that Eastern Shore Animal Shelter is in, I haven't been able to stop thinking about it."

I kneel next to Cosmo and Rocket, and they jump in my arms for a snuggle.

"These two fluff butts wouldn't be a part of our family if it wasn't for that shelter. They rescue so

many animals, and now none of them will get to find a loving family and a home they can play in."

Marie scoffs. "You mean a home they can play anywhere but the beds, the couches, the chairs, the new rugs, oh, and—"

"Point taken, Marie." Mom side-eyes Marie, and they both grin that identical half smile.

"Well, I want to do something to help."

"We're listening," says Dad. "What did you have in mind?"

"Well, it's not completely planned out, but I'm sure Sam and some other friends would help with a fund-raiser. Sam and I spent some time at the dog run the other day, and I think we could babysit dogs there on the weekends while the owners are eating at nearby restaurants. That way, the dogs get their exercise, and their owners get some time to themselves."

"That could work," says Mom. "You'd be serving people who love pets, so they can spread the word about the shelter."

"I'm glad you think so, because I'll need your help if this is going to work."

"I'm in," says Mom, patting my back.

Dad gives my fist a bump. "Me, too."

We all look at Marie, who, for once, isn't staring at her phone.

She shrugs. "Every superhero needs a sidekick. I guess you can be mine."

"Why thank you, my hero, Marie." I toss a throw pillow at her, and she can't help but laugh.

"But seriously," says Marie. "Those dogs are lucky to have you."

The truth is, I feel lucky to have them.

"I'm not sure if we can save the shelter," I say.

"But I'm glad I have the support to give it a try."

I smile and join my family on the couch. Mom puts her arm around my shoulders and passes me the popcorn. "Sometimes all you need in this world is a little hope."

HOPE'S TIPS

When I joined JFK Middle's Science Club, one of the most important discoveries I made was the power of my own voice.

Real talk: Speaking up can be scary at first. Expect a few butterflies in your tummy and for all eyes to be on you for a moment. I know, pretty intense. But once it's over, be ready to feel proud. You're doing a good thing for yourself. Remember, you deserve to be heard. And if there's one thing I've learned from Galaxy Girl, it's that taking on tough challenges can lead to the sweetest victories.

Here are some tips on how you can use your voice, too!

Speak up: Your voice adds so much to the conversation. So join the discussion and share your thoughts. Plus—bonus!—talking breeds understanding and builds connections. So take a deep breath, and say the words you're probably already rehearsing in your head.

Listen up: We all know the courage it takes to speak up. So when someone has the floor, listen and be respectful. Everyone deserves to be heard.

Act confident: Feeling shy? As my mom likes to say, "Fake it 'til you make it!" Try channeling a bold bestie or courageous cousin, or take a pause to clear your throat—that usually does the trick for me. Your audience will be less likely to interrupt when you speak with authority.

Be an ally: I appreciate Camila and Grace backing me up when others kept interrupting me. You can show the same support to your friends. Whether it's a single voice or a chorus, speaking up when others are being mistreated sends the signal that negativity will not be tolerated.

Don't give up: Just because someone didn't hear you the first time, doesn't mean you should give up. And just because you were nervous, doesn't mean you shouldn't try again. Dust yourself off, and keep speaking up. When you use your voice, it's a win for girls everywhere. I'm rooting for you!

About the Author

ALYSSA MILANO began acting when she was only 10 years old. She has continued to work in both TV and movies since then, including hit shows like *Who's the Boss?* and *Charmed.* Alyssa is also a lifelong activist who is passionate about fighting for human rights around the world. She has been a National Ambassador for UNICEF since 2003, and she enjoys speaking to students in schools around the country about the importance of voting. She was named one of *Time* magazine's Persons of the Year in 2017 for her activism. Alyssa lives in Los Angeles with her husband and two kids. This is her first children's book series.

About the Author

DEBBIE RIGAUD is the coauthor of Alyssa Milano's Hope series and the author of *Truly Madly Royally*. She grew up in East Orange, New Jersey, and started her career writing for entertainment and teen magazines. She now lives with her husband and children in Columbus, Ohio. Find out more at debbierigaud.com.

About the Illustrator

ERIC S. KEYES is currently an animator and character designer on *The Simpsons*, having joined the show in its first season. He has worked on many other shows throughout the years, including *King of the Hill, The Critic,* and *Futurama.* He was also a designer and art director on Disney's *Recess.* This is his first time illustrating a children's book. Eric lives in Los Angeles with his wife and son.